TRIPWIRE

Brian Garfield is the author of three widely successful and quite different novels all published in 1972. *Relentless, Death Wish* and *Line of Succession*. Reviewers hailed him as one of the most devastatingly effective and entertaining writers of fiction in the 70s. He is the author of some fifty books ranging from Westerns to novels of espionage, intrigue and terror.

Also by the same author,
and available in Coronet Books:

Deep Cover
Death Wish
Line of Succession
The Threepersons Hunt

Tripwire

Brian Garfield

CORONET BOOKS
Hodder Fawcett, London

First published in Great Britain by
Coronet Books 1976

The characters and situations in this book are entirely imaginary and bear no relation to any real person or actual happening

Printed and bound in Great Britain for
Coronet Books, Hodder Fawcett, London,
by Hazell Watson & Viney Ltd,
Aylesbury, Bucks

ISBN 0 340 20149 5

Perhaps Handy McKay will
understand why this is for
Don Westlake

chapter one

1

When the riverboat came in sight at the bend of the river Boag got up and kicked Wilstach awake.

Wilstach grunted and sat up grinding black knuckles into his eye sockets. "The hell, Boag."

"That yonder's the *Uncle Sam.*" Boag pointed down to the mud-colored river.

Down past the shelf of the bluff the Colorado moved along heavy, swelled with the spring runoff. The riverboat churned along with a good deal of racket and effort but it was barely making headway against the current. Boag had a good view of the sturdy shape of the captain up on the Texas deck; it was near half a mile downstream but the sun was hard as brass and all the shadows had black edges.

"Let's go along," Boag said. "Saddle your jackass."

"Want my coffee first."

"John B., I swan."

"Hell Boag, we got plenty of time. She can't be making three knots."

"Saddle your jackass." Boag turned to the portable heliograph. "I ain't about to miss out. We show up late in Hardyville, Mr. Pickett won't likely wait for us."

He squinted against the sun to set the heliograph mirror at

its proper angle. The mule and the jackass kicked their hobbled feet against the hardpan. There was no wind; the dust settled just where it was kicked up. Boag was coated with the fine powder as if he had been lying for days like Lazarus in an open grave. It was a fine silver grit in the pores of his dark skin and the threads of his cavalry-blue pants. It was abrasive in his teeth and eyes. It made the heliograph's shutter scrape when he flicked it open and shut.

He flapped the handle half a dozen times for dots and dashes. Wilstach was saddling the jackass, muttering about his coffee. After a little while Boag saw the glimmer of the answering signal from the mountain twelve miles northeast of the river, and he batted out the coded flashes for U-S-A-M. He got his winking acknowledgment from the mountain and began to pack up the heliograph.

Wilstach had the jackass rigged. He was throwing the saddle onto the mule. "All I got to say is, that gold better be there."

"You think maybe it flew away someplace all by itself?"

"Boag, you ever seen that gold with your own eyes?"

". . . . No."

"Well then."

"It's there," Boag said. "Close to a troy ton."

"Because Jed Pickett said so?"

"Because they keep four armed guards in shifts on that express-company pier." Boag strapped the heliograph case and heaved the instrument up onto the cantle of the mule's saddle. The thing weighed eighty pounds; he lifted it with one hand. He was big enough to do that.

Wilstach went to the jackass and cut its hobbles. Boag climbed astride the mule. "Come on, you lazy nigger, let's go steal that gold."

2

It was a fifteen-mile ride to Hardyville and it would take Boag and Wilstach close to three hours; Mr. Pickett and the rest of them had a couple of hours' head start but Boag wasn't worried. The gold wasn't going anywhere until the riverboat reached Hardyville and that wouldn't be until the middle of the afternoon. He set a pace that would conserve the animals.

It was all broken wastes on both sides of the river up here, the country buckling and creasing up toward the Black Canyon Gorge a little way above Hardyville, and the Grand Canyon beyond that. The Colorado River came down a thousand miles through the Rockies from somewhere in Wyoming and by the time it got to this point in Arizona it was moving fast and carrying a great deal of mud. It had another four hundred miles to cross between here and the Gulf of California; those were the navigable four hundred miles, and even so the Johnson-Yaeger riverboat fleet only made it up as far as Hardyville during the high water of the spring thaw and the fall rains. The rest of the time the town withered beside a half-dry riverbed and had occasional contact with the rest of the world by way of the Jackass Mail on its way across the Mogollon route from Santa Fe to California. Pretty soon the railroad would reach the Colorado—end-of-track was already as far west as Prescott—but right now Hardyville was about as alone as you could get, between riverboats.

There were a dozen gold camps in the mountains, inhabited by fools who didn't know the hardest of all ways to earn gold was to mine for it. Hardyville was smarter than that. Hardyville let the miners sweat the ore out of the ground; Hardyville just smelted it and stacked it up on the pier and shipped it out to the banks three or four times a year on Johnson-Yaeger paddlewheelers. For performing that service Hardyville made more money out of the gold than the miners did.

Hardyville was a clever hard town that wasn't going to make it easy for Jed Pickett to steal its bullion. Boag had known that from the outset. He hadn't been too eager at first.

That had been six weeks ago in Ehrenburg. The town was building a road to somebody's chicken farm and had adopted Boag and Wilstach the day they arrived there: ten dollars or thirty days, apiece. Boag had a gold eagle in each boot, the last of his mustering-out pay, but he wasn't ready to spend his last twenty dollars on fines for the both of them. They elected jail where the town would feed them. Then they found out about the road.

Good luck it had been early March. Ehrenburg in the middle of the summer would have cooked a man on the road.

On the chain gang they had met Gutierrez, who was a crickety little Mexican with a dewlappy face. Gutierrez let them walk into it all by themselves. He didn't say much of anything at first, he just let Boag and Wilstach complain themselves right into it:

"Boag, what we gon do when we get off here?"

"Cross the river to California."

"Then what? Go back to busting horses for six bits a head, busting our own black skulls in the bargain? Dig graves for a quart of whiskey a corpse?"

"We'll do better'n that. We're soldiers."

"Fine Boag, you just show them your sergeant's stripes and they gon make you the head of the bank."

"We can get jobs riding shotgun."

"Boag, you been in the Cavalry too long. How many white men you know gon trust a nigger to guard their money?"

Gutierrez insinuated himself quietly. He didn't make a big show of his sympathy. "You both got discharged out of the army, hey?"

Wilstach said, "Well we run down Geronimo for them and since then they ain't had enough Innuns to go around. I guess the War Department decided it was easier to feed an Innun than fight him."

"You both in the Tenth Cav, hey?"

Boag said, "That was a lot of miles ago."

"So they just used you up and threw you both out like an old shoe."

"Boag here had fourteen years worth of hashmarks. You see the stitch-marks on his sleeves there."

"How about you?"

"Me I only done six years in the Buffalo soldiers."

"You both kill a lot of Inyuns, hey?"

Boag and Wilstach just looked at the Mexican and he didn't talk to them again for two or three days.

Gutierrez got out two days ahead of them but when Boag and Wilstach were turned loose by the sheriff on the edge of town with four-bits apiece spending money, courtesy of the Town of Ehrenburg, along came a buckboard with Gutierrez driving. "Climb aboard."

"What's all this?" Boag said.

"Amigo, you want a ride up the line or you want to wear out your cavalry riding boots on them stones?"

"Up the line to where, Gutierrez?"

"I got some friends want to meet you."

"Why?"

"I told my friends you two had strong backs. I watched you work that rockpile on the road."

Boag and Wilstach exchanged glances. Wilstach said, "I ain't no pack mule for a Mex outfit."

"Ain't no Mex outfit. Man name of Jed Pickett, maybe you know him."

Boag said, "I heard the name. Scalp hunter."

"That was before," Gutierrez said. "They canceled the bounty down to Sonora, you know."

"Ain't that a shame now," Wilstach said.

"Come on," Gutierrez said. He was sweating under his hat. "Let's get moving, make a breeze on ourselves."

"What's Jed Pickett want with us?"

"We need a couple spare hands. You want to climb up or stand there? I'm fixing to move."

Jed Pickett had a good campsite back in the hills a mile east of the Arizona bank of the river. There was shade under a dozen cottonwoods and a trickle of water out of a hole somebody had dug in the dry creekbed. Boag counted twenty-seven horses on the picket line and eighteen men whose evidence met the eye: bedrolls, saddles, moving human shapes. Maybe the nine spare horses were for pack-saddle work or maybe they were trade-off mounts.

So Pickett had nineteen men, minimum, counting Gutierrez and himself. "What the hell's he need with two more men? You people planning to go to war?"

"You talk to Mr. Pickett, he'll explain."

"Thing is," Wilstach said, "I don't see no other black faces down there."

The buckboard rutted down the hillside toward the cottonwoods. Gutierrez said, "Now listen here. I spent twenty-one days on that chain gang just to pick up men for Mr. Pickett. I didn't enjoy it a whole lot. You two don't work out here, my twenty-one days is wasted. Mr. Pickett ain't gonna like that and I ain't neither."

"Now I could get all broke up about that," Wilstach said. "Couldn't you, Boag?"

"You two," Gutierrez said in a friendlier voice, "was the only ones out of that whole chain gang I thought was worth bringing to Mr. Pickett. That ought to mean something."

"We're here," Boag said. "We may as well hear what the man has to say."

Five men who looked as if they might have helped burn Lawrence, Kansas, stood at the edge of the cottonwoods with rifles in their crook'd elbows when the buckboard came down into camp. Boag made them out to be a Mexican and three hardscrabble whites and an Indian, possibly Yaqui. This was a mixed gang of the kind you didn't find much in the Southwest; the kind of gang you found usually in Mexico, which was sensible since that was where the gang had come from.

The five rawhiders grinned at Gutierrez with five shows of bad teeth. Flat curious glances scraped Boag and Wilstach. Gutierrez said, *"Hóla, chingados,"* by way of greeting to the five men, and the buckboard lurched into camp past them.

A man stepped out of the big tent. Big bones, Boag noticed. A leather face and brown hair thatched over his eyes, large hands covered with brown hair and a pair of revolvers cross-belted at his hips. From the man's eyes Boag judged he was not Mr. Pickett; to boss a crew like this you needed harder eyes than those.

"Ben Stryker," Gutierrez explained. *"Segundo."*

Boag didn't stir but it was good to have his judgment confirmed.

Ben Stryker made a half-turn away from the buckboard as it stopped. "Mr. Pickett sir," he called.

The tent flaps parted and a man emerged, straightened from his stoop and put his contemptuous stare on Boag and Wilstach. "This all you could find, Gutierrez?"

"Good men, you said. I could find plenty of the other kind."

"Shit," Mr. Pickett said. He spat the word out as if it were a fly that had buzzed into his mouth.

Mr. Pickett's face was rough and pitted and as motionless as a professional gambler's. He had a stiff blond mustache. He wasn't an oversized man. He flicked a sideways glance at Ben Stryker who loomed a head taller. "What do they call themselves?"

"You could ask us," Wilstach said. "We got tongues."

Boag sat on the buckboard seat in no hurry to get down. Gutierrez was descending to the ground apologetically. Stryker said, "Mr. Pickett don't like to look up at a man he's talking to."

"Then he'll have to grow two feet," Boag said and stepped down. He was taller than Stryker and a lot taller than Mr. Pickett.

Mr. Pickett said, "All right, you've got size and a tart tongue. What else can you say for yourself?"

"Nothing until I know what kind of auction block I'm on."

"You know who I am?"

Boag had already reviewed what little he knew about Mr. Jed Pickett. During the war Mr. Pickett had ramrodded a guerrilla column in the Border States, a stringer for Bloody Bill Anderson, but that had been twenty years ago and men got older and sometimes soft where they sat and soft where they did their thinking. Mr. Pickett didn't seem that kind, but he'd been a two-bit leader of two-bit men long enough to get arrogant. Down in Sonora they'd put a fifty-dollar bounty on Apache scalps and Mr. Pickett had been one of the gringo bounty-hunters who had made a living off that until Boag and the rest of the Tenth under General Crook had run Geronimo to ground. So Sonora had canceled the scalphunters' bounty and the Jed Picketts were out of work just like the Boags and Wilstaches. It did give them something in common and that was why Boag had come along to see about all this.

"I know who you are," he answered.

Gutierrez said quickly, "These two both Tenth Cav, Mr. Pickett. The big one was a sergeant."

"Then they know their way around horses and guns." Mr. Pickett fastened his unfathomable eyes on Boag. "What do you go by?"

"Boag."

"You?"

"John B. Wilstach."

"Line trooper?"

"Corporal," Wilstach said with his rowdy little grin. "Corporal five times and busted back to line trooper four times."

"Boag, you have a front name?"

"Just Boag." They'd called him Sergeant for a first name so many years he'd forgot about the real one. Leave it forgot, he decided; it had never done him much service.

"You both in the Sierra Madre with Crook?"

"Aeah," Wilstach said.

It seemed enough to satisfy Mr. Pickett. He turned back to his tent and lifted the flap. "Fill them in, Ben."

Stryker went over to a half-dying campfire and indicated a black coffeepot. "Want any?"

"If you ain't got nothing stronger," Wilstach agreed.

"Tequila in my bedroll, you want."

"Yeah," Wilstach said, "yeah."

"Boag?"

"Tequila's fine." He hadn't had a drink in thirty days and more.

Stryker broke out the bottle and passed it around. They were all mighty friendly here and Boag suspected every bit of it.

Stryker explained about the gold bullion in the express-company office on the Johnson-Yaeger pier in Hardyville. "It's been all winter since the last riverboat made it up the river that far. They got a lot of gold waiting."

"How much is a lot?" Boag said.

Pickett's men had drifted through all the camps above Hardyville in the hills. When they'd put all the bits and pieces together it began to look as if the camps had delivered a lot of tonnage of raw ore to the smelter in Hardyville and when you discounted exaggerations and rumors it still looked to add up to pretty near a ton and a half of bullion.

Wilstach said, "What's a ton and a half worth?"

"Say three hundred thousand dollars official price. A mite more down in Mexico." Stryker lofted the half-consumed bottle. "Buy a good deal of tequila for a share of that kind of money, boys."

Boag said, "All right, now you get to tell us what a share amounts to."

"Well you boys are kind of latecomers. Some of these men been riding with Mr. Pickett ten years or more."

"John B.," Boag said, "I don't believe I heard the man answer my question, did you?"

"It'll be good," Ben Stryker said. "Real good for hired-hand wages. It's just one job of work for you two boys and then you take your shares and split up. Be a few days' work in it for you, that's all. We'll be pickin' up a few more men along the line too. Mr. Pickett totes it up we'll need around thirty men to handle Hardyville and that riverboat crew."

"John B., did the man answer the question yet?"

"If he did it must've been in some other language, Boag."

Boag knew why Stryker was taking his time. He was sizing them both up and trying to guess how little they'd be willing to take.

Boag said, "I'll save you the trouble doing sums in your head, Mr. Stryker. John B. and me will take ten thousand between us."

"Mr. Pickett was thinking more along the lines of five thousand."

"Apiece," Boag said.

"Together," Stryker corrected.

"Thirty men, three hundred thousand dollars, that's ten thousand dollars a man. We'll take half that. Seems fair."

"No," Stryker said. "It don't seem fair." He got up and left them alone with the half bottle of tequila.

Wilstach looked around the camp. Nobody was in earshot. Boag contemplated the bottle but refused it when Wilstach offered it.

Wilstach said, "I ain't eager, Boag."

"Why? Don't you think they can get away with it?"

"Sure they can. But that don't make it right."

"Five thousand rights a lot of wrongs, John B."

"Apiece?"

"Together, the man said."

"Then you're inclined to take it."

"I guess I am," Boag said. "What else we got to look forward to?"

"We do this, we maybe could get jerked to Jesus, Boag. You ever seen a man hanged? Flop like a fish on a hook. Man I don't aim to end up right now in Boot Hill with dirt in my face."

"You rather herd sheep, John B.?"

"I would if I knew how."

"Now there's the point," Boag murmured. "What do we know how to do, except soldiering, when push comes to shove?"

Wilstach gave it thought. Finally he said, "Maybe you're right."

When Stryker came back and saw the bottle was empty he said, "You're in, then."

"Aeah," Wilstach said.

"Twenty-five hundred apiece."

"Right," Boag said.

"I'm kind of glad you agreed to join up," Stryker said. "Otherwise we'd of had to kill you. Couldn't have you two tracking around loose knowing what you know."

Boag said, "That gives a man a nice warm feeling, Mr. Stryker."

3

The Johnson-Yaeger express company had an office on the pier, at the shore end of the dock. Tickets for passage were sold here, and shipments added to bills of lading. The warehouse for shipments was on an adjacent pier but the gold was held in the first building, probably because it was easier to guard: the building was small, it was exposed on all four sides, and it had only two doors, front and east side. There were windows here and there but they were barred with heavy cast-iron grilles bolted through to the inside of the timber studs. The front door gave access to the ticket window inside; behind the ticket counter was another wall with a door in it that led through to the back room where the gold was kept. That interior door had two armed sentries on it and the outside side door had two more. But there was more of a problem than that. The armed sentries weren't all that formidable by themselves. The town was.

Hardyville was a town of armed citizens all of whom were aware of the gold in the Johnson-Yaeger office, some of whom owned shares in it, and a few of whom might be willing to die to protect it. No one could say how many would fight, but the gold belonged to the town as a whole so if you wanted the gold you had to be prepared to fight the whole town.

Johnson-Yaeger had built its express office on the pier deliberately, not only because it was the nearest place to the riverboat landing but also because it was surrounded on three sides by the bulk of Hardyville. From the office it was a seven-block gamut in any direction before you reached the outskirts. So you either had to run that gamut or swim, or use a boat. The only boats in Hardyville were the skiffs used by Californians to cross the river, and none was nearly big enough to carry a ton and a half of gold bullion. In fact all of them together couldn't carry it.

The way Mr. Pickett had it worked out, the time when Hardyville felt safest was the time when the riverboat came and collected the gold and took it away. At that point the gold was no longer Hardyville's responsibility.

But that was also the time when the gold was easiest to take.

Boag tied his mule to a rail in front of the Bella Union saloon. He left the heliograph on the saddle because he didn't expect to need it again. He had a two-pound revolver under the skirt of his campaign jacket, rammed in his belt just aside from his spine. He walked the two blocks from the Bella Union to the Johnson-Yaeger pier, not hurrying, drawing a few incurious glances from pedestrians. Traffic was light on the street but what there was of it was converging slowly toward the riverboat pier because the rumor had gone around that the boat was due in this afternoon.

There was a knot of people around the waterfront when he got there. He posted himself in some shade across the street from the Johnson-Yaeger wharf and watched the fast brown river lash itself against the pilings. The sun was west of zenith and made painful reflections on the water.

He spotted Gutierrez and Stryker in the crowd, milling aimlessly, pretending they didn't know one another. Gradually during the next half hour a dozen of Mr. Pickett's rawhiders came along singly and by twos and melted into the throng awaiting the *Uncle Sam.* Empty freight wagons began to appear, drawing up at dockside ready to unload the flat-bottom hundred-foot vessel when she berthed.

He saw John B. Wilstach come down the street on his jackass and tie up in front of the assay office. A little while later the crowd's mutter began to grow into a roar and he saw Mr. Jed Pickett walk in sight around the corner of the Inter Ocean Hotel, and that was the sign that the riverboat had been sighted from the roof of the hotel.

Wilstach was over near the express office and when he caught Boag's eye he flashed his grin, filled with its rowdy flavorings. Boag pretended he didn't see Wilstach. None of them was supposed to know any of the others.

Boag was thinking of ways to spend his twenty-five-hundred dollars. You didn't just piss that kind of money away. You went to a town somewhere where they didn't mind the color of your skin too much and you opened an establishment. A saddlery and blacksmith shop, he figured, because he'd been enough years in the Cavalry to know everything you had to know about repairing tack and mending gear and shoeing horses.

It wasn't much of an ambition but then ambitions were new to him and he was feeling his way. In the army you just did your forty miles a day on beans and hay and you let the War Department worry about ambition; once you got your sergeant's stripes you were as far up as a nigger soldier was ever going to get, but there was nothing wrong with being topkick of a good line troop of Buffalo soldiers, a man didn't need any more ambition than that.

Now he was thinking vaguely in terms of Oregon or the British Columbia country. Need to get a long way away from this part of the world after today. And up in western Canada he'd heard around the barracks that they didn't piss on black skin.

Boag was slow to hate, his temper took a long time rising, but he was getting ready to hate the army for what it had done to him.

The steam whistle shrieked across the desert and the crowd got up on its toes. The *Uncle Sam* wasn't in sight yet; there was a last bend for her to come around.

You needed manpower, Mr. Pickett had explained to them all, and you needed to time it right. There would be a point when the ship was just about completely unloaded—

that would be just short of sundown—and at that point most of the ship's crew and the longshoremen-for-the-day would be ashore, and that was the point when you had to strike. It would take most of the twenty-eight rawhiders to hold back the crowd on shore while the rest moved the gold on board the boat and got the drop on whatever crew was left there.

"Moving the gold aboard," Stryker had told Boag, "that's you new boys' job."

It put Boag and Wilstach and the rest of the new recruits at the bottom of the gang's ladder, but Boag was willing to be nothing more than a strong back for a day, for twenty-five-hundred dollars in gold. You had to spend five years in the army to earn that much pay and you never saw more than forty dollars of it in one hunk.

The tall structure of Uncle Sam hove in sight with the paddles grinding away at the water, straining; the current along here ran pretty close to sixteen knots. Boag tipped his shoulder against the weathered clapboard wall and settled down to wait.

The clerk in the Johnson-Yaeger office was a weary man with his hair all wet down, a bony pale man wearing sleeve garters and an eyeshade. Boag stood across the doorway from Wilstach, looking in. Two men were booking passage on the downstream leg; the clerk was chastising them for being tardy. "Most everybody booked two, three weeks ago."

"You got room or ain't you?"

"Deck passage only, Mister. You stand up all the way unless you can find a wagon to sleep under."

"I'd stand barefoot on hot coals all the way to Yuma to get out of this God-forsaken country."

The two men got their tickets and left, coming out between

Boag and Wilstach. One of them brushed Boag's shoulder and turned his head quickly, ready to apologize until he saw what Boag was. Then his face tightened. "Jesus Christ. Don't you know no better'n to get in a white man's way?"

Boag lowered his eyes. The man said, "You want to learn better manners, boy," and hit Boag in the belly.

Boag let it cave him in. He sagged back against the wall holding his stomach in both hands. "Yes sir I sure got to learn better manners sir."

"Christ you niggers ain't worth the powder to blow you to hell." The man turned to his partner. "You coming?"

His partner was bent over against the building because he was laughing so hard. Finally the two of them moved away.

Wilstach simmered. "I had my druthers—"

"Forget it, John B. It don't mean nothing."

"Tomorrow," Wilstach said in anger.

"All right, tomorrow." Boag watched the two men walking away. Not walking; swaggering. Wilstach was right. Tomorrow. . . .

Ben Stryker approached in his clawhammer coat. "Smart," he murmured. "All set? Come on—it's time." And the three of them went into the office, Stryker pulling a shotgun out from under his coat and talking softly to the clerk and the two guards on the interior door. "All right, don't get notions. Stand still and nobody gets theirselves hurt."

Gutierrez backed into the room behind them and Boag heard the door click shut.

"Lord Jesus," the clerk said. "Road agents."

From the set of Stryker's dreamy smile Boag knew enough to feel sorry for the two sentries if they even thought about being brave.

They didn't. They let Wilstach take their guns. Stryker stood guard with his shotgun, his eyes half closed in wedges; the clerk and the two sentries sat down on the floor behind the clerk's counter and Gutierrez held them there at gunpoint while Stryker went to the door and opened it and made hand signals in the twilight, and soon seven men came through the door and helped Boag break into the back room.

"Christ," one of them said, "I wish to hell it was greenjackets instead of that stuff. Look at how much that stuff weighs."

It was piled on pallets in stacks up to a man's waist, four pallets—pyramids of gold bars stacked up crisscross like loose bricks. In the poor light it glistened. Boag's breath got hung up in his throat.

"That's fine," Stryker was saying. "Nice and quiet."

Boag looked over his shoulder and the dockside was calm: nobody had noticed anything. Yet.

"Throw all that on one buckboard, you gon bust the wagon," Wilstach warned.

"We use two wagons," Stryker said. "Here they come—get back from that door, hey?"

Boag heard the splintering crackle when crowbars broke the outer padlock hasp. The outside door of the freight room yawed open and two men, sentries, backed inside with their hands in the air. Three of Pickett's old-timers came in prodding them with guns and after they had a quick look around the room one of them went back to the door and called outside:

"All rat, brang up 'at wagon."

There was the loose rattle of buckboard tires against the dock planking. Stryker said, "Start heftin', boys." Boag reached for an ingot and went to lift it off the stack and nearly lost his balance. It was as if the thing was nailed down with railroad spikes.

"Jesus."

Stryker said, "That's what you boys here for. Bend your backs."

Boag grinned at him and heaved. He got the gold bar off the stack and tucked it under his right elbow and heaved a second ingot up in his left hand and carried the two of them out the side door to the buckboard.

But he was breathing hard when he came back for the second load.

5

Eight of them moved the buckboard to the ship's gangplank—Boag and two others on the yoke, pulling, and the other five at the back of the wagon with their shoulders to it, hauling up on the back spokes of the rear wheels. This was the risk part because now the whole damn town saw what was happening.

There had been a lot of argument back in camp because Stryker and some of the others didn't see why you couldn't just let the Johnson-Yaeger crew load the gold onto the boat themselves. That was where it was going anyway. But Mr. Pickett had ruled that out. The gold was generally one of the last things loaded aboard the ship because it had to be one of the first things unloaded at the Yuma end of the voyage. By the time they would have waited for the express company to carry its own weight aboard, the ship would have been crowded with passengers and crew. That was no good, Mr. Pickett said. The boat had to be as nearly unoccupied as possible.

It wasn't just that it made a lot of sweat-work. It was that the whole town would see it happen.

That was why, Mr. Pickett had explained, you had to have a thirty-man army to carry it off.

Now Boag was heaving on the wagon tongue and the rest of them were yanking and shoving and the heavy wagon was creaking up the slight pitch of the gangplanks to the low-riding main deck of the *Uncle Sam*, and back at the shore end of the wharf Mr. Pickett's men were strung across the pier in an armed line with shotguns and rifles holding back the curious and the angry. Hat peaks showed along most of the adobe and shingle rooftops: those were Mr. Pickett's men too, their rifles stirring constantly so that everybody in the buzzing crowd knew there was a gun on him. Citizens were hurrying to and from the waterfront with ideas and plans and the news. The crowd got bigger and bigger and its noise became higher-pitched, hotter.

"*Heave.*"

The wagon lurched onto the deck. Boag dropped the tongue and they all reached for ingots. Boag said, "Don't nobody drop one of these, likely it'd go right down through the deck."

But there wasn't time for making neat stacks. They just set the bricks down by the wagon in a heap and then they were dragging the wagon off the ship and shoving it off the side of the pier to make room for the new buckboard that was already half loaded with ingots back by the company office. The empty wagon floated a few yards downstream and got wedged on a sand bar. Boag and Wilstach were on their toes, running. Inside the office they shouldered into the trio of loaders and lent a hand finishing the wagonload. The light was very bad by now and Stryker had refused to light a lantern in the gold room—"You want to be an easy target?" They had to load the last bricks by feel.

They started to wheel the buckboard down the pier and a flurry of gunshots erupted. Boag threw himself flat on the planks. A bullet screamed off one of the gold bricks. Mr. Pickett had a surprisingly big voice for a man his size: it was calling across the wharves. "Get that damn fool." There was a fusillade of shots, mostly from Mr. Pickett's outposts on the rooftops, and Boag saw a man fall out of the second-story window of the assay-office building, and somewhere in the crowd a man started to scream; there was another volley of shots from overhead and the scream was cut off abruptly in its middle.

A ragged aftervolley, and things calmed down; the citizens were scrabbling for cover and the waterfront streets were emptying.

Somewhere back there in the town the local defenses were organizing themselves and it wouldn't be long before an army of locals came charging down the alleys filled with determination and brimstone. There wasn't a whole lot of time. Stryker was bellowing: "*Heave.* Damn you lazy bastards!"

Boag was heaving; he caught the flash of Wilstach's grin.

Mr. Pickett went forging past them up the gangplank at the head of a wedge of his men; they were heading straight up for the pilothouse on the Texas deck, where a couple of the men already had guns on the captain and the helmsman There was another Pickett man in the engine room and now when Boag's boots reached the gangplank he felt the heavy throb of the mechanisms under his soles.

Mr. Pickett's sharpshooters were making their way down from the rooftops. Now another firecracker series of gunshots began: That was Mr. Pickett's men, retiring, firing the occasional shot to keep the townspeople's heads down. In the darkness the rifles shot out orange lances of flame. Boag had his fingernails clawed into the splintery wood of the buckboard tongue; he backed up the gangplank, his back arched over, hauling. The sharpshooters began to swarm up along the pier and a few of them lent their shoulders and finally the wagon was bumping onto the deck.

Stryker was talking: "Never mind unloading the damn thing. Somebody lash it down where it stands. Use a couple of them shore lines—there's cleats all along the rail there. . . ."

Half Stryker's words got eaten up in the explosions of gunshots. The town had rallied and a crowd pressed onto the wharf blazing away at the boat: there was a lot of hysterical calling back and forth, a lot of confusion and rage; they were shooting into the Uncle Sam because they were too stupid to realize if they sank the riverboat it would cost more to replace her than the value of the gold they were trying to save. But bullets were punching through the woodwork and shrieking off the brass, and Boag threw himself flat into a companionway and lay there, streaming sweat.

Men were running along the deck and he heard Stryker somewhere: "Cut those fucking shore lines!" There was a high grinding racket as the paddlewheels began to roll; that was Mr. Pickett up in the wheelhouse with his gun muzzle pressed against the Captain's throat.

Boag fished the revolver out of his belt and went to the corner of the companionway but he didn't fire any shots; he had nothing against the townsfolk. *Just keep your big ass out of sight, Boag.*

The Uncle Sam was easing out now. Citizens in stupid panic were running out onto the pier firing their guns and Pickett's sharpshooters on the high Texas deck were picking them off with cool calculation. Three or four of them flopped down on the pier before the rest got smart and wheeled for cover.

The riverboat backed into the current and began to turn her nose downstream; the Colorado picked her up and swept her away from the lights of Hardyville. After a bit Boag put his revolver away and went looking for Wilstach.

He found Wilstach at the rail just aft of the left-hand paddlewheel housing and Wilstach didn't look happy or even relieved. Half a dozen of Pickett's old-timey rawhiders were clustered loosely around Wilstach and three of the other new hands that Stryker and Gutierrez had recruited. Gutierrez was there, emitting the hoarse laugh he always barked out when he was nervous, and Stryker was coming down the stairs from the Texas deck behind two more of the new hands, a pair of Yuma Indians they'd recruited coming up along the riverbank last week.

Stryker said, "This most of them?"

"All of them," Gutierrez said. "We left four back on the pier." The nervous laugh. "I reckon the town's having fun with them right about now."

After that there was an ugly little silence as Stryker came down the stairs to the deck. Boag saw it shaping up and thought about ways to handle it. He started to edge back into the deeper shadows but Gutierrez had fast eyes: "Come on, Boag."

Wilstach said, "Hey . . ." because he suddenly saw it too.

Then the dark banks were rushing past on both sides of the ship and outlined against the sky at the head of the stairs was Mr. Pickett, his strong voice breaking the throbbing night: "Get it done, Ben."

"Yes sir," Stryker said. "All right now, you boys right over the side."

Stryker hadn't even showed his gun but there were a dozen of them up on the rail of the hurricane deck, watching.

"Aw you rotten bastards," Wilstach said wearily.

Boag picked up sudden movement in a corner of his vision —Gutierrez whipping out a knife behind Wilstach. Boag tensed to move but Wilstach had seen it too; Wilstach wheeled, whipped his hand up and caught the knife descending: it razored into his palm but Wilstach twisted, snapped it out of Gutierrez's fist, and took the hilt in his left hand to stab. Wilstach's hand flashed with the knife and when Gutierrez swerved to parry the threat, Wilstach kicked him brutally in the crotch.

Stryker was bawling: "Hobble it! Hobble it!" in his twanging voice but nobody paid him any mind. A high reckless joy filled Boag's chest and he waded in toward Gutierrez but then two of Pickett's rawhiders were right in front of him with knives.

"Carve them up," Pickett bellowed.

Boag knocked one of them aside backhanded and grabbed the second one and got the knife away and stuck it against the man's throat.

Boag threw his head back. "Mr. Pickett."

"What?"

"You want this little ballet to continue, Mr. Pickett, I'm going to have to kill this man here."

"Well I wouldn't do that Boag, because if you kill Sweeney you'll get twenty men to sit heavy on you. Now you just turn loose of him."

Sweeney struggled in Boag's grip and Boag pricked the point of the knife against Sweeney's Adam's apple. It quieted him down. Boag backed slowly over to the rail. "Come on, John B."

"You gon jump, Boag?"

"I am."

"Without our shares?"

"How you gonna swim with gold bricks?"

"Well shit," Wilstach complained, but he broke away from Gutierrez and came over to the rail. Gutierrez snarled a little and then cackled nervously again.

Sweeney stirred again and Boag let him feel the point of the knife. Sweeney was big enough to make a good shield. It was the only reason they weren't shooting at him.

Mr. Pickett said, "Go on then, get over the side. I'm tired of looking at you."

Boag reached around behind him left-handed and fumbled the revolver out of his belt but as soon as it came in sight, Mr. Pickett backed away from the hurricane rail, out of sight.

Boag glanced at Stryker, at the foot of the stairs. Stryker had a gun out. Boag thought about shooting him but it wouldn't change anything if he did. None of them cared that much about Sweeney's hide; they'd sacrifice him. There just wasn't any way to win this one. Finally Boag said, "Go on over, boys. Ain't no choice."

There were the two Yuma Indians and there was a new white hand who called himself Frailey. And there were Wilstach and Boag. These five were the ones Mr. Pickett had no further use for.

The white one, Frailey, climbed over the rail and Boag heard the splash when Frailey hit the water. Boag said, "Go on," but the two Yumas shook their heads and Boag understood. They couldn't swim.

That was when Sweeney kicked back hard. His bootheel caught Boag in the shin. Sweeney dived away and Boag was standing there right out on the bare-ass deck and there was nothing to do but flip himself back over the rail.

6

The guns started up before he hit the water. The pain in his shin and the shocking cold of the water made him lose his grip on the revolver; for a moment he was strangling in the foamy froth kicked up by the bucketing paddlewheels, a black swirl of panic; he kicked and heaved with his arms and none of it seemed to do any good, there wasn't any up or down. He hadn't got much of a breath in his chest when he went over; he didn't even know if he'd been shot or not, but everything seemed to be in working order except his sense of direction. He was tumbling ass over teakettle in a marbled darkness of water which had no top and no bottom. *Christ I don't want to drown.*

The water was up in his nose like fire; he was strangling. He flailed in madness and there was a slow burst of white-hot agony in his chest.

Then his boots rammed something solid: the bottom, a rock. He let his knees sag and then he made a leap, shoving himself up from the bottom.

His head broke the surface instantly. The Colorado was a very shallow river.

He coughed and wheezed for breath. The turbulence of the boat's passing afterwash wheeled him around. The moon spun crookedly and then he picked up the boat with his eyes, the ruby gunflashes from along the rails. He saw it clearly when Pickett's men shot the two Yuma Indians and threw them over the rail.

Then he spotted Wilstach, swimming strongly toward him against the current. Bullets made spouts and creases in the water and Boag filled his lungs and coughed and finally shouted, "Get your head down!" before he dived under and fought the current toward the near bank.

He stayed under as long as he could. Came up for air and had a look around to get his bearings. He was a little closer to shore than he had been; the riverboat was farther away, a good hundred yards downstream now. The guns were still volleying in flashes. Wilstach's knobby head broke water between Boag and the *Uncle Sam*; Boag shouted something and went back under.

His hand touched bottom and he started dragging himself along the sand bottom. The current skidded him along. He would get a fist into the sand and propel himself sideways across the current and then the river would push him downstream ten feet.

It was shallow enough to walk it now, but if he did that they'd target him against the pale clay of the sloping banks. He stayed under and crawled until his lungs caught fire.

When he put his head up for air he saw them shoot their last volley. *Uncle Sam* was disappearing around the bend. Boag got his feet under him and stood angled back against the current, and searched for Wilstach.

He saw arms flail the surface. It was Wilstach but he wasn't swimming strongly any longer; he was batting the water weakly. It was due downstream and Boag just kicked his feet loose and let the current carry him along, breasting with his arms to add speed. But before he reached Wilstach the arms and head disappeared under.

Boag swam harder.

They must have put a bullet into Wilstach and if Wilstach let the current carry him around the bend they'd have him in sight again from the high deck; the moon was plenty good enough for shooting. Boag had to find him first.

Then he saw Wilstach come up for air, one arm flopping up. Boag reached him and grabbed the arm and dragged him in to shore.

But John B. was dead.

chapter two

1

He sat on the ground dripping, filled with agonies, out of breath. He was too spent to think, but when he heard footsteps in the brush he levered himself to his feet ready to face the next challenge.

It was Frailey, the one who had jumped overboard ahead of them. He was walking downstream, his feet squelching in his wet boots.

"Well then," Frailey said. He seemed too tired to say anything else for a while. He sat down and put his eyes on John B. Wilstach who lay where Boag had dropped him on the bank. The river rushed by with a steady racket and bugs whined around Boag's ears but he had no strength to bat them away.

"What happened to him?" Frailey asked stupidly. Boag didn't bother to make any answer. Finally Frailey said, "You ain't talking?"

What was there to talk about?

Frailey said, "Never knew a coon didn't go stupid-ass silent when it was convenient."

"Shut your mouth." Boag felt in his pockets. "You got a couple of copper pennies on you?"

"What for?"

"Put on his eyelids."

"If I did I wouldn't give them to no dead coon."

"If I had a Book I'd read over him. You know the words?"

"No. If I did I might have to read over both of you."

"What?"

Frailey said, "You caught one or two yourself, I see."

Boag looked down where Frailey was looking. Against the matted wet darkness of his pants a couple of darker spots were starting to show up.

He'd thought it was just the lingering pain from where Sweeney had kicked him.

"Got a knife on you?"

"No," Frailey said. "I got nothing but the clothes on my back. I'm as dirt-nigger poor as you, right now."

"Well I ain't gonna die from that," Boag said. He got both hands on the pants cuff and ripped it up to the knee and rolled the cloth back gently; it was already starting to stick to the wounds.

They'd put two bullets through his right calf. Not through the bone. The blood was a slow ooze so it was vein blood. The bullets must have gone straight through. He twisted his leg around and saw where they'd come out the back in the soft fleshy part of the calf. Probably cut some muscles up. The exit holes were wider than the others and the two had coursed together into one ragged bleeding wound.

"You maybe ain't going to die from it," Frailey said, "but you sure as hell ain't going to walk very far on it for a while."

Boag untied the bandanna from around his neck and wrung water out of it and tied it around his calf. He'd seen enough battle injuries to know you had to keep it clean and you had to keep quiet until the scabs built up. If you did those things there wasn't much danger in it.

He sat and brooded on John B. Wilstach for a while. Finally Frailey said, "Tell you what, I'll get a stick, scratch a hole for him."

"That's mighty kind."

"No. He's liable to start to stink in the morning. Bring a lot of buzzards down. Draw everybody in Hardyville down here to find out what's happening. I can't get far enough on foot if they start a search."

Boag lay on his side listening to the river and the bugs. The leg throbbed and he watched Frailey make a trench grave for Wilstach. There was a great deal of dried blood in the palm of Wilstach's hand where he'd twisted the knife away from Gutierrez. Wilstach didn't look dead, he looked calm and pleased with himself; a couple of teeth showed where his lips were open a little, and he looked as if that rowdy grin was about to flash.

Boag said, "Hey."

Frailey paused in his labors. "Yeah?"

"Mr. Pickett said he knew where he could sell that gold in Mexico."

"Did he?"

"You got any idea where in Mexico?"

"Naw. I wasn't even with them as long as you was." Frailey started to dig again but then he stopped and straightened up and looked at Boag. "Shit, you ain't thinking of going after them?"

"They owe me."

Frailey let out a bark of laughter. Then he went back to his digging.

Boag said, "How much did you have coming?"

"Twenty-five hundred, same as you."

"Then they owe you too."

"Coon, when you've played enough cards you know when it's time to take your losses and go look for another card table to swill at."

"Well maybe."

"Old Frailey's just going to move on, give some other place a potshot at me." Frailey stopped digging and looked up across the river. "California over there. Maybe find me a stake and a card game."

Frailey seemed to judge he'd dug deep enough. He threw the stick aside and walked over to Wilstach. Boag said, "If you're thinking about stripping that dead man you can forget it. He ain't got nothing on him."

"I wish he had a hat. I could sure use a hat." Frailey picked up Wilstach's bootheels and dragged him over toward the grave. "Boots are a lot too small for you or me." He rolled the body into the hole and picked up dirt in his cupped hands and gradually Wilstach disappeared from view under the mound of soil.

Afterward Frailey went down to the river and washed his hands off, took a drink and stood a while looking at the far bank. "California," he said, and the word barely reached Boag's ears over the tumble of the river. In the end Frailey said, mostly to himself, "Well my boots are still wet anyway," and walked out into the river until it was up to his neck.

The river was about a quarter-mile wide. Boag watched Frailey swim across, the current carrying him ten feet downstream for every two feet headway he made; he was almost out of sight beyond the bend when he waded up on the far shore, a small figure in the moonlight. He didn't turn or wave or anything. He just walked up into the bush willows and disappeared.

2

He slid himself down to the river. There was no hurry. He soaked the bandanna to get it as clean as he could and then he had a closer look at the wounds. He picked a few small pieces of grit out of them. They were still bleeding a little and he made compresses out of ripped pieces of his shirttail, washed them and fitted them into the wounds and tied the bandanna around them, tight but not tourniquet-tight. He left the compresses in place fifteen or twenty minutes and then he removed them and was satisfied to see the bleeding had stopped, at least on the surface. He tore off a few bits of frayed skin and then lapped the openings together as well as he could while he brought the bandanna up around his leg again and tied it firmly.

Now it was best not to move for a while. You had to leave the wounds alone for the raw edges to start to knit together.

He heard an owl talking in the cactus somewhere uphill of him. That made him feel a little better because it suggested a way to get food but right now it was sleep he needed and he lay flat seeking it.

But sleep was hard to come by. There was thinking to do, there was emotion to accommodate.

He spent a long time remembering John B. Wilstach whom he had known six years and partnered with for three, in the army, and half another year since mustering out.

Then he was thinking about Gutierrez and Sweeney and Ben Stryker, and mostly about Mr. Jed Pickett with his big voice and his stiff blond mustache. Of course they hadn't planned to cut Boag and Wilstach and the other new hands in at all. They'd just wanted strong backs to move the gold for them while they used their rifles and shotguns to keep the town of Hardyville at bay. Boag and Wilstach and Frailey and those two Yumas and the rest of them had been pack animals to Mr. Pickett, nothing more than pack animals. When you were done using a pack animal you turned him in or turned him out. Mr. Pickett had left half his pack animals in Hardyville for the citizens to play with and he'd thrown the other half overboard after shooting the two Yuma Indians to death and trying to kill Boag and succeeding in killing John B. Wilstach. There were white men who did that kind of thing for sport. Nobody had shot Frailey; Frailey was white and Frailey took a white man's view of it—a bad turn of the cards so Frailey would forget it and move on.

So they'd been shooting at Wilstach and Boag in the water not because there was any real reason to kill them but just because it was fun to shoot at moving targets.

Falling off to sleep Boag wondered if Mr. Pickett knew what it was like to be a moving target that somebody was shooting at for fun.

3

By daylight the gunshot ugliness in his leg was annoying: there was no point putting his weight on it yet because that would bunch the muscles and tear the things open again. He dragged himself around slowly doing what had to be done: a drink from the river first, and then up the bank until he came to a game trail in the brush where animals came down to drink. That took more than an hour although he found the game trail within a half mile of John B.'s grave. He spent two hours breaking sticks and honing them against rocks to make a figure-four trigger of branches on top of which he balanced the biggest stone he could claw out of the ground and roll up the bank on his knees. If a deer came along first it would be bad luck because the deadfall wasn't tall enough off the ground and the deer would just knock the thing over. He had to hope the first drinkers after dark would be maybe badgers or a 'possum.

If it didn't work there was always that owl he'd heard in the night. The owl would hunt in its own bailiwick and when Boag heard it make its kill he would scare the owl off its meal and steal his supper. There was also the river but Boag didn't like fish much.

The banks were crowded with arrowweed and rushes and the occasional stunted scrub willow. It was a long day's work breaking branches but by sundown he had a pile big enough to suit him. Then he crawled back to the grave and exhumed John B. Wilstach.

The smell was bad. Boag stripped the clothes and belt off his friend and left John B. in the grave with nothing but his boots on, and covered him up again.

He tore the clothes in strips and used most of the strips to tie the bundles of branches into something that approximated a raft. Then on one knee he lugged himself back up to the game trail to find out what his deadfall had snared.

He didn't expect much of anything and he was ready to go

around following that owl half the night, but he ran into a little luck. The deadfall had killed a small porcupine.

You used a lot of care with porcupine. He rolled it over onto its back after he got the rock off it, and jabbed a broken twig into its throat and laid it out along the bank with its head downhill. He worked the twig in and out until he had severed all the main arteries.

While the blood drained he spent twenty minutes honing the steel edge of Wilstach's U.S.A. belt buckle against the flat side of a rock until he had a blade on it. He slit the porc's belly from chin to tail and peeled the flesh back, removed the innards and used the buckle-knife to separate the meat from the pincushion hide. He only got three or four quill pricks in his hands.

There hadn't been any sign of pursuit along the riverbanks but it would be stupid to build a fire and invite investigation; he wasn't more than ten or twelve miles south of Hardyville. He ate the meat raw.

4

The current carried him along at a good clip and only occasionally he used the oar he'd built like a broom by lashing a bunch of stiff rushes to the end of a broken willow limb. When the sun started to get hot he soaked Wilstach's bandanna in the river and tied it down over his head. Every little while he took it off and wetted it down again. No point getting sunstroke. He remembered the white officers of the Tenth and their tired jokes about the Buffalo soldiers' suntans.

He had worked it out in his head. It was about 375 river miles to Yuma and the current held a steady twelve- or fifteen-knot speed down the Colorado. Taking an average that meant he would be about thirty hours on the river. He'd lost some blood and there was still the vestige of shock; he couldn't expect to spend fifteen hours a day steering the raft so he gave himself three days.

He was already thirty-six hours behind them when he started, and the steamboat would pick up another day on him—maybe two days—but still they'd only be three or four days ahead of him out of Yuma and they had the weight of that ton-and-a-half of gold to slow them down. They'd have to use pack mules or wagons.

He didn't have a plan worked out. That would come.

In the middle of the day he let the raft drift onto the sandbank in a bend by the western shore and he rested a while and ate the last of the porcupine meat that he was going to eat; there was some left but it would go rancid by nightfall and he kept it with him only to use as bait for fishing. He made hooks out of the metal eyelets of the buttons from Wilstach's shirt-tunic and he said, "John B., you're helping me catch up to that son of a bitch all the time." Slender strips of Wilstach's clothes made his fishing line and he tied Wilstach's brass buttons just above the hooks to attract the eyes of the fish. He imbedded the hooks in porcupine meat and let the lines trail the raft and by sundown he had six little fish aboard.

He had come far enough to risk a fire; he built one Indian-style and rubbed willow sticks over arrowweed tinder to start it going. He disliked fish anyway but raw fish was too much to contemplate; he cooked them in their skins and cut them open afterward and ate them from the inside out, spitting out the bones, hungry enough not to mind the taste.

The leg was mending all right. He still hadn't put his weight on it and he didn't intend to until he had to. Things were coming along, he thought. He'd need a gun and a horse but he still had the two gold eagles in his boots and that was enough to buy a gun and some cartridges, and with that he could commandeer the rest.

"I know it, John B., it's a damn fool thing to be doing. But

I got nothing else to do right now and I never expected to make old bones anyway."

The next morning the current took him into an eddy of rapids that smashed up his raft and almost drowned him and busted his leg wounds open all over again.

5

The sun had both feet on his shoulders. Above the rock banks the desert winked and glittered with pyrites; heat haze wavered above the ground. When his head cleared he looked ahead across the long curve of rocks and pebbles. No reed bottoms here, it was all rock and then withered sand country above that. Nothing to build another raft with. The muddy flow of the river rushed through the sands.

A single wagon stood sagging on the near bank just below the bend.

Boag tied up his leg and started forward on one knee and both blistered hands, moving with the careless deliberation of half-drowned exhaustion.

The effort sapped him less than halfway along and he had to lie down in the sun for a time; and that was when he heard something stir.

He rolled over on his side and dug for the sharpened belt buckle in his pocket. His eyes swept the rocks in a steady arc.

A flutter of brown movement drew his attention to the left. A ragged small figure emerged from the boulder and stared at him with large grave eyes: a scrawny little girl in a filthy sack of clothes.

She spoke to Boag in Spanish, in a piping high voice: *"Quién es usted?"*

The little girl came toward him without fear. Boag said in Spanish, "How many of you over there?"

"There is just me. And then there are the Mexicans."

"How many?"

"Who are you?" she said again.

"Corazon," he said, "I do not have time to fool with you. How many are the Mexicans?"

"The old man and the woman, that is all." Her eyes were bottomless and held distrust but not fear. Her skin was the color of old copper; she had a narrow triangle of a face and black hair tangled with burrs. Anywhere from nine to thirteen years, she had. Boag said, "You're Indian."

"I am Yaqui."

"All right."

"You are a *ladrón,*" she told him.

He started to drag himself toward the wagon. The little girl buzzed around him like a horsefly. Finally Boag got to his feet slowly. It was the first time he'd stood up in several days and the blood fell from his head; he tightened his belly muscles and waited for the dizziness to pass. Finally he hobbled toward the wagon, putting very little weight on the bad leg. "You look like a stinking Gypsy to me."

"I am Yaqui," she said angrily.

She kept worrying close to his heels while he stumbled along the rock bank toward the wagon. "Don't dog me," he said.

"Why should I obey a *ladrón negro?* Have you killed many men?"

Boag hobbled to the wagon. The old man and the fat woman sat in its narrow band of shade and the old man had a Spanish percussion rifle aimed at Boag.

Boag stopped two paces from the rifle. "Put your rifle down, old man."

The old man looked sick; he was sitting still but his chest heaved with his breathing. His face was lined as though he had slept all his life with his face pressed against a screen of rabbit wire.

Boag bent down, gripped the rifle and pulled it out of the old man's limp grasp. It had not been cocked and it did not go off. Boag slung it across the bend of his elbow. "If you point a gun at a man it only makes good sense to cock it."

"We have very little ammunition left," said the old man. He sat against the wagon wheel and soon the sun would reach its midpoint and either the old man would have to suffer its rays or he would have to move underneath the wagon. He seemed to drift; his eyes kept closing slowly and popping open again. He wore dust-coated remnants of good Spanish clothing, old now, worn thin and patched.

The fat woman said, "He has the fever," as if in apology.

"He has chills?"

"Frequently."

"When the chills start you should cover him up. Keep him covered and get all the water down him he can swallow."

Her eyes beseeched. "Is that all one can do?"

"What do you want me to do? Hold his hand?"

"Will he be better?"

"He'll be better or he'll be dead." He turned. "You ought to tell that little girl to wear a hat in this sun."

Boag sank down in the patch of shade beside the old man. "What happened to your mules?" The iron rim of the wheel was hot against his back.

"Two Mojaves came here the night before last night," the woman said. "They ate our meal with us and then stole our mules and our cow."

"No mules," Boag said weakly. He roused himself: "How do you expect to get anywhere without mules, you damn fools?" But it was in English, this last, and they only gave him puzzled looks, the woman and the girl; the old man's eyelids had sagged and he wasn't listening. Boag wiped a forearm across his face and looked at the river and saw that this had been a ferry landing at one time. The wreckage of a ferry-raft was tied up on the far side of the river.

Thc wind came damp and sultry off the river. He was thinking that old wreck of a ferry would make a good enough raft if he could find some kind of pole to steer it with. Maybe that wagon tongue of theirs.

The old woman had got started and seemed unable to stop talking now. "We have seen much misfortune. The revolution has destroyed my husband's properties. We must go to my uncle in California, in the county of Tuolumne."

"What revolution?"

"In Sonora the revolution."

They were always having revolutions in the northern provinces but he hadn't heard about a current one. "Tell me about that."

"How can I tell you anything while my husband is so ill? We must get him across the river. This desert is a poor place for a proud man to die. He must be brought to our family in Tuolumne."

The wagon's stripe of shade was very thin. Boag said, "You'd better get him under the wagon."

He sat frowning at the river while the old woman struggled with the old man's weight. "*Niña,* come and help me."

The little girl moved reluctantly; they struggled and the old man tried to assist them but he seemed weak to the point of helplessness. It was curious he had been able to hold the rifle.

The old woman sat down by Boag. "There is no one to rob here except ourselves, and we are poor, it would not be worth your trouble. You must either go back in the desert or swim across the river. But you cannot go back, for you have no horse. What happened to your horse?"

"You will hurt yourself talking so much."

"I have nothing to do but talk, and you have little to do but listen. You cannot return into the desert with that injured leg. You must swim across. I only ask that you carry the end of the rope and tie it to the ferryboat. When you have done that, we can pull the ferry across to us."

"You have a long enough rope?"

"We have three *riatas* and if they are tied together they are very long."

"You are mistaken. Three riatas would be two hundred feet, perhaps three hundred feet of rope. From here to the other shore is four times that distance. Perhaps more."

"There must be a method," she said with stubborn helplessness.

"What if I say you can die without my help?"

"Then that is what we shall do, is it not?"

"What if you do get to the far side? You still have no mules."

"But we shall be in California then."

"What difference does that make? It is still the same desert."

The old woman seemed puzzled and confused. He saw that she had been doing the same thing Boag had been doing for several days: thinking ahead just one step at a time because if you thought it all the way through you had to give it up. The old woman had thought no farther than the other side of the river.

He could get across the river by himself all right. The old ferry would be an adequate raft.

Boag crawled down to the ferry landing. The flies were numerous but he paid them no mind.

When the little girl came down to the dock Boag laid his hand on the rifle. "You're a witch. Get away."

The little girl said, "They keep me because I can work but they hate me because I am Yaqui and they know the Yaqui is better than they are. You are a *ladrón,* you can understand. My father was a warrior and he killed many of them."

"And they killed him, didn't they?"

The little girl ran away. Boag picked up the rifle and hobbled back to the wagon. The wound wasn't as bad as he'd feared this morning; he felt better about the idea of a swim across.

The old man was breathing heavily beneath the wagon, a flush on his cheeks. The little girl wandered away into the rocks.

The woman said, "The truth is that her mother was not a Yaqui. Her father may have been. A mountain thief, I am sure."

"Your mouth flaps," Boag told her.

"Would you shoot me for that, tough one?" A plump finger waggled at him. "You will not shoot, but you will leave us to die."

"Old woman, I have trouble enough of my own." He made his way down to the river. The flow was fast and steady, and frightening. He bounced the rifle in the circle of his fist.

Finally he went back to the wagon. "Listen to me. I will take you to Yuma—I go that way anyway."

If the woman had feelings she gave no indication. "How will you do this?"

"Swim across, pole the ferry over to this side. The current will drive me far downstream before I reach this bank so you must get him on his feet and come down along the bank to meet me."

He went back down to the crumbled landing and scowled at the river. This morning it had almost killed him.

The little girl trailed him there. Boag had the rifle in his fist and the little girl said, "You cannot take that with you."

"You are right."

"I will keep it for you."

He didn't trust her, but he trusted her not to be able to use the rifle. He handed it to her and stepped into the water. His toes felt the suck of the mud bottom. He stepped out again and stripped off his pants and shirt and placed them in a neat bundle on the landing. "Bring these to me also."

"All right, *ladrón.*"

The sun was very hot on his bare flesh. He moved out into the current, feeling the force of the river against him. It rushed warm toward the south. He struck out into it.

In Boag's judgment they made seventy miles before nightfall. Delay annoyed him but the old man was too weak to make a night trip of it. They camped in reed bottoms.

Boag lay on his back with one knee bent and the Spanish rifle across his stomach. After the fire was laid the little girl came and sat beside Boag and talked softly. "If we go to California the old man will die, and she will have her people. They will have no use for me."

"Then you will have to learn to look out for yourself."

The woman propped the old man up against the raft and they ate. The food was meager. Afterward Boag picked a spot to sleep, and did not awaken until sunrise. In the morning he had a look at the leg. Swollen but not much pus; the scabs were tight, the leg itched. Good signs.

The old man lay on his back, his mouth open and slack. Boag looked away with his eyebrows drawn together. He pitied them all and he was angry because he had to be pitying them; they were getting in the way.

The sun blasted his face. Heat glistened on the muddy surface of the Colorado and the water rushed past the banks, tearing bits of it away.

The woman crouched by the old man. "He is dead."

They buried him in the riverbank. The old woman mumbled words and Boag filled in the grave and tamped it with a stone.

"That was kind," the woman said.

Boag grunted.

"But there are still the three of us," she said.

"No, there are the two of you and there is the one of me."

"And we are not three? You have no sums?"

"I have no ties," Boag said. "I'm a fool. I ought to let you get across the river by yourselves, the old man did."

"And now you are a philosopher? Besides, we no longer go across, we go down the river, yes?"

"Yuma is as far as I go with you."

"That is understood."

The little girl waited until the woman went away to kill the fire; the little girl said, "She will sit in the sun in Yuma and die."

"She doesn't care about you, *niña*. Why think about her?"

"She does. She is only gruff."

"I thought you hated her."

"I do."

"Make up your mind."

"What are you going to do after we come to Yuma?"

"Leave me alone," he growled, and set his good leg in the mud to shoulder the ferry-raft into the river.

7

By the next night he was tired of them both, tired of the little girl's chatter and the woman's sour body smell.

In the dusk he poled the ferry-raft through the crosscurrents of the Gila fork. The Gila rose somewhere in the mountains over in New Mexico or far-eastern Arizona and came down the White Mountains, fed by the Salt River and some others, and went past Phoenix and a few no-account towns and finally flowed into the Colorado here a few miles north of Yuma. Buffalo-soldiering, Boag had followed the pilgrim highway along the south bank of the Gila a good many times across the desert. It was nobody's favorite river.

He got the raft through the turmoil and they floated on down. Boag said, "You said you would tell me about the revolution in Sonora."

The little girl watched them both with her big angry eyes. The woman sighed. "They are a people who must be slaves or tyrants. Revolution only means exchanging one group of tyrants for another."

"Who are they this time?"

"Pesquiera is the governor. There are bandits and rebels trying to overthrow him."

"Who leads these bandits and rebels?"

"Why do you ask?"

"Just tell me, *vieja.*"

"I think it is a man called Ruiz from Caborca. I am not sure. There are many bandit chieftains who pretend they are revolutionary leaders."

"What does Mexico City do about all this?"

"No one in Mexico City cares what happens in the provinces. We beseeched the government to help but they ignored us, which is why we are without our properties. The *peones* burned us out and ran to the hills to join the bandits who promised them freedom."

It sounded familiar enough to Boag. The woman said, "But there is no freedom for them except for the few who become tyrants."

"Who's going to win?"

"Who can say? The Governor Pesquiera has many troops, he will probably win."

It was dangerous making too many guesses. But a man like Mr. Pickett would find some way to make profit out of rebellions. Yet right now that didn't necessarily follow: Mr. Pickett had three hundred thousand dollars' worth of gold bullion and he didn't need to mix in anybody's trouble for money right now.

A ton and a half of gold. It had to leave deep tracks. Boag kept dwelling on that.

And here's Boag without a cent in his kick. Well there was still the twenty dollars in his boots, he hadn't lost that.

The raft swept around a wide bend and just beyond the tall bluff sprouted the lights of Yuma town. There was a big prison on the bluff, of which Boag had heard tell; he didn't want to get anywhere near that, he'd had enough of jails in Ehrenburg. He poled the ferry-raft up onto the eastern bank of the river in the darkness a quarter mile north of the town. "I get off here," he said. "You can get this raft to Yuma by yourselves or you can walk."

The woman gave the raft her dubious attention. "We shall walk, I think."

The little girl was watching them. She hadn't said a word for quite some time and that was unusual if not unique.

Boag helped them unload the few possessions they had salvaged from their wagon. He still had the old Spanish percussion rifle which he considered a moment before he proffered it to the woman. "You can sell this for the price of a meal and a telegraph wire to your people in Tuolumne."

"You have been kind."

"You will find help in Yuma, it is a big town."

The river picked the raft off the bank and moved it out. It spun slowly into the muddy flow.

"You two go on ahead," Boag said.

"And what of you?"

"I got things to do."

The little girl snatched at Boag's hand. "My name is Carmen."

The woman snorted. "She dreams. Her name is Pilar, *Señor.*"

"I wish to be called Carmen."

"All right Carmen." Boag managed a bit of a smile before he pulled loose of her grip. *"Hasta luego."*

"Adiós," the woman said, and smiled showing the gaps between her teeth. "Go with God, our good friend."

The woman started off laden with her things, the long rifle sticking out above her shoulder. The little girl didn't stir and finally the woman came back and rearranged her load to free a hand, took the girl by the arm and pulled her away.

Boag watched them fade into the dissolving darkness against the lights of Yuma. When they were out of sight he began to limp along toward town.

chapter three

1

He dusted himself off as well as he could and decided he probably wouldn't draw any more attention than any other black drifter on the night streets of Yuma. He was clean enough; he'd bathed several times the past few days, in the river with fire ashes and grease for soap. It was the clothes that were bad: ripped here and there, caked with river mud at the cuffs. He'd have to get clothes. It wasn't vanity, it was the knowledge that they arrested you on appearance more than anything else and if you looked reasonably prosperous they'd leave you be. It was the ragged army uniform that had betrayed him in Ehrenburg, there were too many mustered-out Buffalo soldiers in Arizona right now and the whole Territory knew they were broke, jobless and vagrant. Nobody trusted them.

Walking into Yuma by way of dark side streets, Boag added up his requirements. Two pounds of iron and a holster and cartridges for it. Clothes. A water canteen, maybe a rope; a hat. A clasp knife surely. A horse, blanket, bridle, saddle. Scabbard and rifle and cartridges. At a minimum that would do it; everything else could come off the land, although it would save him time later if he found a pack of jerky and tinned food to carry along.

He toted up the value in dollars and knew he was nowhere near cutting it with his two gold eagles. A handgun, a decent .44-40 or .45, was twelve dollars right there and that was more than half his stake; a repeating rifle would run twenty all by itself.

You could stop and earn the money doing day labor but it would take months.

Well you could steal a horse, maybe a horse with a traveler's pack on it, and then you could steal guns and clothes here and there. But then you'd have half a dozen victims looking for you along with the sheriffs.

There was one other way and it looked better than the others.

Boag stopped in an alley and worked his boots off and got the two small gold coins out. Put them in his pocket and felt around to make sure there wasn't a hole in that pocket, and squeezed his feet back into the boots and walked on down the slope between houses, his eyes and ears guiding him toward the town's fandango district.

The lamps were bright along the strip of whorehouses and saloons. A steady traffic of pedestrians thickened the mud-caked sidewalks and every saloon had a crimson-faced barker out front hawking the pleasures of the place in a strident voice. A great deal of cheerful racket; and here and there a gambling loser prowling through the crowd with his hands rammed in his pockets and his face twisted up in angry defeat.

Boag had thought of trying his hand at a gambling table but he wasn't all that good at it and had dismissed the idea instantly.

He picked a dive smaller and more poorly lit than most of the others. He pushed inside through the crowd on the porch. The place had no door, only a doorway. That meant it was probably open around the clock. It must have been one of the oldest buildings in Yuma: it was a narrow dark little 'dobe with a low ceiling and improbably thick walls, and the stucco had peeled off parts of it to expose the chipped adobe bricks. The bar was a simple affair of planks laid across big empty beer kegs; a pair of Mexican bartenders moved sweating up and down the backbar slot. There were no mirrors or chandeliers. A few oil lamps on the walls, flickering on insufficient oil, and two ceiling-hung lanterns above round card tables where players sat in candy-striped shirts and laborers' coveralls. One poker, one faro. Scrape of chair leg and bootheels, chinking of coin, clink of bottles against glasses, lusty voices; the place was thick and close, redolent of spilled whiskey and stale beer and used tobacco smoke. The floor was scuffed adobe and boots had worn a trench in it along the base of the keg-line of the bar.

Boag bought a five-cent beer and saw the barkeep make a face when Boag presented a ten-dollar gold piece; Boag took his beer and his change and went over to the back end of the bar to eat the free lunch that came with the beer. The sandwich bread was stale as overcooked toast and the slices of dry beef had curled up at the edges but it was nourishment and he chewed steadily while he put his attention on the faro rig.

The rigger was sliding cards out of the faro box, intoning "Queen loses, six wins." They were playing for two-bits a card and Boag switched his interest to the poker table, moving along the back wall to bring it in focus and then standing backed against the 'dobe, thumbs hooked in his pockets, keeping to the shadow where he wouldn't draw attention.

The game was table-stakes pot limit with a four-bit ante. There were six players around the table, playing with varying degrees of interest and intensity. Boag singled out a middle-sized man whose face had a shape and texture that reminded Boag of heaped walnuts in a wooden bowl. The man played carelessly, without a great deal of attention; obviously he was playing to pass the time and didn't much care about the game, but he was getting a good run of cards and in the first ten minutes Boag saw him rake in two fair kitties and one forty-dollar pot.

One of the others addressed walnut-face: "You finding enough good cards tonight, Elmer. You put the Indian sign on that deck?"

"You know I had it in mind to try cheating you boys,"

Elmer said cheerfully, "but when you all sat down to play I saw I wasn't going to have to. 'Scuse me a minute, save my chair. Deal me out one hand." Elmer went over to the bar to buy another drink and the player beside him put his boot up on Elmer's chair to keep anybody else from sitting there.

When Elmer returned to his chair Boag settled down to watch the game and wait it out.

Elmer said, "Lee Roy, when you aim to get delivery on that cherrywood bed I ordered?"

"Should of been here by now. I can't say. You know the way things get, coming across. They had to ship it out of Boston and probably it got held up wagoning acrost Panama. Then they bring it up to San Pedro on an ocean steamer and they transfer it onto one of the Johnson-Yaeger steamers up there, and it got to come all the way back around below Baja California and up to the mouth of the Colorado and then they got to transfer it again over onto one of the riverboats. I mind that rocking horse Mrs. Watson ordered from Baltimore took eight months getting here. You just never can tell."

Boag sipped his beer and watched with his eyes half closed. A man who could afford to order a cherrywood bed shipped from Boston wasn't poor.

One of the other players said, "Hey talking about steamers and all, what the hell happened to the *Uncle Sam*?"

Lee Roy said, "What you mean?"

"She was due in yesterday. Still ain't showed up. My cousin Brill supposed to be on board, comin' back down from Hardyville. I hear he made two thousand on pelts this season. Man we want to rope him into this poker game, he shows up."

"Well two days ain't much overdue," Elmer said comfortably. "I raise you three dollar, Sammy."

"Fold," Lee Roy said. "I wouldn't worry much. She might of got hung up on a sand bar. Sometimes takes them three, four days to work loose of them sand bars in the river."

"I call," Sammy said, "give me two cards."

Now that gave Boag something to think about. The *Uncle*

Sam hadn't showed up in Yuma yet but Boag hadn't passed her anywhere on the river and he'd come all the way down by raft behind her. He'd expected they would probably ram right through Yuma on the river and keep going right down to the estuary of the Colorado, which was in Mexico and out of Arizona's jurisdiction. But she hadn't come through. Now where the hell did you hide a hundred-foot paddlewheel steamboat?

It took him fifteen minutes' thinking but he finally worked out how they must have done it, and that made him feel better. A good deal better because it meant he wasn't as far behind them as he had feared.

He watched Elmer's stake grow steadily for two and a half hours until Lee Roy suddenly stood up and pressed both fists into the small of his back to lean back and stretch. "That's it for me, Elmer, your luck's running too good tonight. I'll see you boys."

It broke up the game. New players started to move in to the table and once three of the original players had left, Elmer didn't seem to see any reason to stay around and let the others try to get even. He scooped his winnings into a canvas poke and pulled the drawstring shut and stuffed the poke down in his hip pocket, finished off his drink—it was the fifth shot of whiskey Boag had seen him down—and meandered out of the saloon, pausing twice to talk to acquaintances. While Elmer was talking to the second one, at the bar, Boag moved slowly to the door and went outside.

It was about midnight and the traffic had thinned out on the street. Boag put his boots down into the loose dust of the thoroughfare and walked across the way to the dark passage between two red-light houses opposite the saloon. He posted himself in the shadows until Elmer emerged from the saloon and when Elmer turned up-street Boag let him get a block away before eeling out onto the boardwalk and following him.

2

At the mouth of an alley Boag caught Elmer from behind, clamped his palm over Elmer's mouth and lifted the revolver from Elmer's holster. Boag jammed it in Elmer's back and hissed in Elmer's ear:

"Eef you don' keep es-shut op, I goeen to keel you. Onnerstan'?"

Elmer nodded and Boag removed his hand from the man's mouth. "Now don' turn aroun'." He lifted the fat poke from Elmer's hip pocket and stuffed it into his own.

"Now you es-start walkeen. Es-straight ahead an' you don' look back, onnerstan'? You look back an' I goeen to hahv to es-shoot you. *Ahora ve.*" He prodded Elmer in the back with the gun muzzle and Elmer walked away unhurriedly, an easygoing fellow who took such things with equanimity. Boag waited until Elmer had traversed most of the length of the alley before Boag wheeled back around the corner and broke into a sprint across somebody's dark lawn.

He slipped through back alleys for ten minutes before he stopped in a passage behind a thriving saloon. Lamplight spilled out of a high back window, enough for him to see. He emptied Elmer's poke and separated the coins from the greenjackets; he distributed the coins in his pockets so that they wouldn't make telltale bulges. The greenjacket bills he stuffed back into Elmer's poke because paper money was printed up by various local banks and Elmer might be able to identify his own greenbacks, although it was doubtful since he'd just won most of them in the poker game. Still there was no point taking the chance. Boag left the poke, the greenjackets, and Elmer's revolver in the pile of trash behind the saloon; guns had serial numbers and Elmer might be able to identify that too.

With one hundred and forty-six dollars in coin on his person, Boag climbed into the loft of a horse-boarding stable near the waterfront and fell asleep almost instantly, his leg throbbing only a little.

3

He had himself clothed and outfitted and ready to go by nine in the morning; by nine-thirty he had ridden beyond sight of the Yuma bluff and was trotting north on the hard-mouthed horse toward the confluence of the Colorado and the Gila.

It was a used McClellan army saddle for which most civilians wouldn't give ten dollars, which Boag had paid for this one; he was used to the split-tree saddle, he'd ridden them nearly twenty years. The rifle was a .38-56 Winchester with calibrated hunting sights and the revolver was a .45 Colt Theuer-conversion model, ten or twelve years old but the rifling grooves and lands were in good shape and there wasn't any rust on it and the gunsmith had let him have it for four dollars. He'd bought ammunition moulds and primers and crimpers as well as several boxes of cartridges so he was ready to reload his own if circumstances took him where you couldn't buy cartridges, especially for the .38-56 which wasn't all that common a caliber. He'd picked it for its high velocity and long-range accuracy; a steady enough rifleman could keep all his shots within a hat-size circle at four hundred yards with this rifle, and that was a lot better than the Army .45-70 he'd been used to, where you were out of luck beyond two hundred yards.

He had a few luxuries like a flint-and-steel fire-starting mechanism, a rain poncho, a good flat-crown border hat, and somebody's old heavy plaid flannel riding coat which might keep him warm if he had to ride up into the Sierra. He had spare underclothes and socks and he'd bought a pair of moccasins which were now in the saddlebags along with several days' worth of food. The canteen was a two-gallon container: heavy, but if you ran out of water in the desert you were dead.

And he still had sixty-four dollars in his new jeans. He'd bought well—all except the horse, about which he was beginning to have his doubts. Thirty-five dollars for a seven-year-old sorrel gelding with the gait of a razorback sow and the mean eye of a wolverine.

But the horse moved along at a good clip and he guessed that would do.

He found the Uncle Sam where he had thought she would be. You couldn't really hide anything that big. They'd put her where nobody would look for her for a while. It was where she had to be and Boag had no trouble.

They had steamed her up the Gila a few miles to a point where the highway veered away from the riverbank and went around behind the far side of a big hill. They'd anchored her up under the overhang of some big cottonwoods. Nobody would come across her by chance; you had to be looking for her to find her. So far, nobody had any reason to be out looking for her.

Except Boag.

Obviously Mr. Pickett had planned it all pretty well in advance. The buckboard was still on deck, they hadn't bothered to use it. Boag examined the tracks leading away from the boat. The horse and mule tracks (he assumed they were some of each although from the remaining indentations it was impossible to tell which was which) were too numerous to count but there had to have been thirty or more. They'd probably loaded about two-hundred-and-fifty pounds of gold onto each pack animal. It made for quite a mule train. But that was a lot more maneuverable than wagons would have been.

He followed the trampled mess up around the hill and across the highway, tracking southeast. It had been some years since he'd been down here on Cavalry patrols but he had no trouble remembering how it lay. A hundred miles of dry soda lakes and baked soil that was scorched and cracked and shriveled by a perpetual drought and a perpetual sun. Tumbleweed and cactus and the occasional mesquite and patches of greasewood and organ pipe. Give this country an inch and it would take your life. You had to shake out your boots in the morning before you put them on because if you didn't you might be putting your toes in with a scorpion or tarantula or centipede or black widow.

He had a look at the horse-droppings. None of them was still moist or green. Hard to say how much wind there had been in the past few days; the extent to which sand had drifted into the tracks was no real indication of how long they'd been gone, but working out the probabilities in his head he judged they had to have three days' jump on him, possibly closer to four.

He tested the weight of the canteen—a nervous gesture; he'd just filled it in the Gila and watered the horse and drunk his fill—and then he gigged the horse out into the Sonora Desert.

4

When the cruel sun climbed high he knew he was going to have to surrender to it and take shelter. His cracked lips stung with sweat. If you kept moving in this blast of heat you'd use up too much water on the horse and yourself. There were waterholes down along the Border but they were two days along from here; you had to ration things. Better to travel the cool hours of evening and night and early morning. There would be a moon again tonight, getting on toward last-quarter; enough to track by.

Somewhere deep underground a rock cistern gathered enough moisture to feed the long roots of a clump of mesquite. He hobbled the sorrel and bedded down under the meager shade. Dust motes hung in the sunbeams that lanced down between the branches. He slept; he had the ability to relax completely when there was nothing to do.

The clock inside him brought him awake when it was cool enough to eat. Somewhere around half past four by the sun.

He gave the horse a ration of water and scrubbed out the old Army mess kit with sand, put everything away where it belonged, saddled the horse and untied the hobbles and went on his way into the evening.

In the night three times he came across the bleached bones of travelers who had tried to make the crossing without sufficient experience.

In places the wind had blown the tracks over completely but it was impossible for a thirty- or forty-horse trail to disappear that quickly; a few minutes' scouting around and he always picked them up again. The trail led him steadily southeastward on the high flats. Mr. Pickett knew exactly where he was headed.

There were a few towns down that way—Sonoyta and some others, scattered around the oases of the plain. Beyond the Border there were mountains and then more desert, although that desert was not as dry or treeless as this one. Mr. Pickett was heading into Mexico as he had said he would. The question was, once in Mexico—where then?

He found shade at nine-thirty in the morning and although it wasn't fully hotted up yet he decided not to risk another few miles; he ate and bedded down and waited out the heat. He was up before four, eating dried beef and pinto beans and the last of the cornbread, and feeding the horse a nosebag ration of grain and a hatful of water. The canteen was less than half full now. He put a pebble in his mouth and rolled it around with his tongue to keep the saliva going.

At sundown he came upon what he had feared he might find. The tracks began to split up.

By twos and threes and fours, groups of horses peeled away from the main gang and went their own way. All of them headed generally southward but the little bunches were diverging by miles. The main track got smaller and smaller and finally there was no way to know which was the main track any more, and at ten or eleven o'clock that night Boag had to toss a coin. He picked a set of four-horse prints and settled down to follow them south.

5

He was guessing but his opinion of Mr. Pickett was that in each group of four-horse prints you would probably find two trustworthy old-time Pickett rawhiders, one pack animal loaded with gold, and one relative newcomer to the Pickett-Stryker organization whose potential greed would be tempered by the constant presence of the two old rawhiders who probably slept in shifts and kept both eyes on him. In that manner Mr. Pickett would guarantee, as much as it could be guaranteed, the safe delivery of that portion of the gold to wherever it was destined.

Splitting up this way would be a risk—three men and a packhorse being far more tempting to bandits than an army of twenty-odd men armed to the teeth—but then it did make the track harder to follow and it also provided good odds that most of the four-horse groups would get through.

It was odd the way he kept thinking of Mr. Pickett's men as old rawhiders. It was the same way he thought of himself as an old soldier. They were mostly in their forties, not old men at all. It was just that they'd been riding with Mr. Pickett for more than twenty years, most of them. They probably averaged six or seven years older than Boag, that was all; by his best reckoning Boag was thirty-seven. In Mississippi they didn't keep close birth records on field niggers. Boag didn't know but that he might be a field nigger right now if the war hadn't emancipated him when he was about fourteen or fifteen by his own reckoning; he had lied about it—he was big, he had always been big—and the Army had thrown him right into its new black horse-regiment, the Tenth Cavalry, because Boag had a natural eye with a rifle and the seat of Boag's pants fit very well on the back of a standard-size Cavalry horse.

They had fought the Sioux on the northern plains and the Comanche on the southern plains and there had been several years' garrison duty and then the Army had sent them out under Crook to find Geronimo.

Then when the Indian wars were over the Army decided to cut back about two hundred personnel. They found in the service records of Boag and Wilstach that they'd both been busted back to private several times for various infractions, so the Army discharged them in the middle of Arizona and they found themselves in the desert with no trade but soldiering, no job but drifting, and the road leading finally to the Ehrenburg jail.

Now on Mr. Pickett's backtrack Boag was thinking about Wilstach and thinking about all that gold. Of course he was just one man and he was a little crippled up by the bullets he'd taken on the river, but he had nothing better to do with his time and you needed some reason to get up in the morning.

There was the revolution going on in Sonora; there always was. Boag expected to have to dodge some combat. In times of rebellion in Mexico anybody suspicious was in danger of getting killed merely as a precautionary measure.

In a midmorning blaze of heat he reached Tanques Verdes where the four horses ahead of him had watered. Under the shade of the towering *algodones* Boag went from the trading post to the blacksmith's stable to the saloon asking questions about the three men with the packhorse. An hour's questioning convinced him that the three men had not been Mr. Pickett or Stryker. As he had guessed there was one relatively young man, a Mexican, and two middle-aged gringos. One of the two gringos had stayed with the packhorse at all times during the six or seven hours the men had spent in Tanques Verdes four days ago. None of them had said anything that anybody remembered about where they were headed. They had eaten supper and ridden into Mexico at sundown.

Boag filled his canteen and replenished his food and rode out after them.

A gauze of dust hung low over the desert. He rode past the heap of stones that marked the international boundary and climbed toward the foothills in Mexico.

The track was vague and intermittent. Winds had blown the prints over, sometimes for hundreds of yards at a stretch.

Boag scowled irritably at the earth and often had to guide on flimsy probabilities: an iron-scratched stone, a carelessly broken greasewood branch where a horse had brushed too close. Every fifteen or twenty minutes he would come across a patch on the lee side of some boulders or brush where the prints of the four horses were still identifiable. He hadn't lost them but he was losing time with all the circling and back-tracking it took to stay with them.

In the past twelve hours he had climbed a steady and barely perceptible incline and was probably two thousand feet higher in elevation than he'd been last night; the difference in sun-temperature was apparent and it was no longer impossible to travel by day. He pushed on through the sun hours and only stopped for half an hour to noon on the north side of a hill.

By now of course somebody back in Yuma would have gone looking for the *Uncle Sam* and probably they'd found her on the Gila but the tracks had had several more days to blow over and it was not likely any posse would take up the hunt. Johnson-Yaeger would complain to the Territorial Governor at Prescott and in due course an official inquiry would be lodged in Mexico City, probably identifying Mr. Jed Pickett, and as usual it would be put into some dusty drawer and ignored. Mexico City was still busy getting out from under all the problems that had been created by the reign of Maximilian and Carlotta and they didn't have time down there to poke around looking for gringo fugitives.

He was relieved not to be burdened any longer by the weighty presence of the old woman and the persnickety little Pilar who wanted to be called Carmen.

Angling more directly south than before, the tracks led him up across foothills into a minor range of mountains with which he was not familiar; the Geronimo chase had not taken the Buffalo soldiers this far west in Mexico. There was timber up here, the ground was covered with a silent lawn of pine needles and the late afternoon sun flickered through the pines like a moving signal lamp as Boag climbed toward the high passes, keening the ground.

It was a hard country for tracking; the pine needles did not take impressions and hold them. But the ground was soft underneath and in bare spots they had left hoofprints in the rotted half-mud. It was one of those open mountain forests with no underbrush; the high corridors ran unobstructed between rows of lanced pines and the air was very cool with a sharp coniferous pungency. Boag's horse moved along with very little sound and for a moment he was reminded of a church he had once rested in, an empty church in some mountain village south of Fort Defiance.

He was hurrying the horse because he knew there would be no tracking after dark in these woods. At sunset he was ready to give it up for the night when he picked up the lights of some establishment winking through the forest and he homed in on them, riding into a little village of log buildings that was decidedly un-Mexican in flavor; you thought of all Mexico as being nothing but mud huts and dusty plazas and narrow streets in squalid colors. This was more like something in the Wyoming mountains. But wherever men went they built with the materials at hand and up here the most plentiful things were pine trees.

Probably a community of trappers and prospectors and those who traded with the mountain Yaquis. There were half a dozen log cabins, cook-smoke rising from the chimneys of three of them, and there was one large building with a galleried porch across the front and a pair of long hitch rails at which Boag counted seven tied horses. All but one had Mexican rigs and there was no packhorse but he hadn't expected to come upon any of Mr. Pickett's people this quickly anyway. The one horse that stood out from the rest had a blanketed McClellan rig and when Boag looked closer he saw the U.S. brand on the horse's flank. An American Cavalry horse, but not a regulation Cavalry saddle. Something to look out for, he judged; he dismounted and loosened the cinches and gave the hard-mouth sorrel a nosebag of grain and climbed the four wooden steps to the porch and walked along the porch to a window to look inside.

It was a trading post with a saloon bar along one of the

walls. He counted six Mexicans standing at the bar eating pinto beans and pork cubes off wooden plates. They were hardcases, their chests crossed with bandoleros of cartridges. The seventh man was a gringo in a fringed buckskin outfit that looked as if it had been made up for a performer in a wild-west show. Boag recognized him mostly by the clothes and by the dirty white Cavalry hat with its crossed brass sabers; it touched Boag with surprise and then made him grin and he walked along the porch to the log door and went in, and the gringo in buckskin looked around with his dour long face—the lugubrious doleful face of a professional mourner—and broke into a painful creasing of wrinkles which passed for a smile. "Well zippity-doo-day if it isn't the good Sergeant Boag!"

"Your humble servant, Captain," Boag said.

"You're a long way from home, Sergeant."

Boag said, "I have to be."

"Tequila or mescal or beer?"

"Tequila, beer chaser," Boag said, and Captain Shelby McQuade relayed the order to the man behind the bar.

"You hungry, Boag? I don't much recommend the food here, it's enough to give a buzzard the trots but there's not a whole lot of competition."

"I could eat, Captain, my belly feels like my throat's been cut. What you doing in this town?"

"I thought," Captain McQuade said, "that question was one that nobody in a town like this ever asked."

"No offense."

"I'm just ribbing you. You're welcome to ask."

"Those boys with you, Captain?"

Captain McQuade looked upon the six armed Mexicans

with distaste. Evidently none of them spoke English; they watched Boag with curiosity, reserving hostility. "They're with me," the Captain said without pleasure.

Boag sampled the tequila. "They seem to be putting bigger snakes in these here bottles this season."

Captain McQuade's mouth smiled again while his eyes sized Boag up. "Looks like you've got some kind of burden, Sergeant."

"Well I'm looking to find some people. How long you been in this town, Captain?"

"About two hours. I gather that won't help you."

"Looking to find three men rode in here maybe four days ago, probably rode right out again."

"Well you can ask the storekeeper here. These three men some kind of special friends of yours?"

"I guess not," Boag said.

Captain McQuade took a snap-lid timepiece out of his pocket and opened it and raised one eyebrow, and put the watch away. Boag said, "You got to be someplace?"

"There's time. Got a bit of a ride ahead of us." Captain McQuade glanced at the row of fierce Mexicans and shook his head and said under his breath, "Been a long time since I closed both eyes, Boag. You wouldn't be looking for a job, would you?"

"Doin' what?"

"Same kind of thing you used to do before the both of us got cans tied to our tails. Only this time you'd be my topkick instead of Captain Gatewood's."

Boag said, very dry, "Which side, Captain?"

"Rebels."

"Ruiz?"

"That's right."

"You hiring out mercenary, Captain?"

"What else is a soldier to do?"

"I don't know, Captain. I ain't sure I understand why you ain't still in the Army. I mean I always thought they couldn't fire officers."

"They can put them on shelves someplace where they

can't do a damn thing for amusement. They wanted to post me to some Godforsaken Indian agency in Texas with a detail of four enlisted men. I don't know a worse way to rot, Boag. I resigned and came here seeking adventure and usefulness and I imagine I've found them. But I can't say I'm happy with the tools I have to work with. I'd be a much happier man if I had a man at my back I knew I could trust. These gentlemen you see here would slit your throat for a peso."

Boag kept his hat on while he ate, standing up at the bar. "So now you're a captain in Ruiz's rebel army."

"Actually I'm a *coronel.*" The doleful eyes beamed.

"Well congratulations, Captain."

"How about it—Sergeant-Major?"

"I guess not, Captain, I got a few fish to fry. But thank you."

"Pays a good wage, Boag. You draw down a hundred pesos every month and that's in gold coin, and on top of that you can keep anything you loot."

"Well I'm obliged but no."

"What are you so bent out of shape about? Somebody step on your sore corn?"

"I guess you could say that. You know anything about Mr. Jed Pickett, Captain?"

"I've heard he used to scalp-hunt around here. Haven't heard anything about him recently. What would you be having to do with the likes of him?"

"Just looking to find the man, that's all. He owes me something."

"I'd forget it, Boag, Jed Pickett's as crooked as a dog's hind leg. You go looking to get him to settle a debt and you're just likely to spend the rest of your life all shot to pieces."

"Well chicken today, feathers tomorrow. I'd dearly like to catch up with Mr. Pickett."

"They'll take you apart and throw the pieces in the Gulf of California. Jed Pickett travels with a retinue, Boag. Fifteen or twenty men and the one that wouldn't shoot you for the fun of it's as rare as a pair of clean socks around an enlisted men's barracks. Why don't you just forget this debt of Pickett's?"

"I guess I just ain't gaited that way."

"Boag, I must admit there have been times I suspected you had nothing but pork fat between your ears. This is one of those times. I recall you always did think with your fists, it got you busted three or four times and this time it's likely to get you killed. Why the hell don't you give it up and join up with me? We can have a hell of a fine time trying to kick over the pail."

Boag mopped up the last of the bean gravy with a crust of heavy bread. "Coffee, Captain?"

"Uh-huh."

Boag said to the barkeep, "Draw two," and turned his back to the bar to hook his elbows over it. "Captain, Mr. Jed Pickett must have somebody around Sonora he deals with when he's got something to sell. You wouldn't have no notions about that, would you?"

"I don't follow you."

"Well Mr. Pickett's got something that belongs to me and I expect he aims to sell it somewhere. Now how would you tote that?"

"Well I think you're a damned fool to pursue this, Boag, that's the way I tote it. But there's a man named Almada down the Rio Concepción a few miles the other side of Caborca, owns a big ranch and a hacienda, and a good many of our rebel bandits go there to trade loot. You might try Almada."

"Much oblige."

"I've got to be moving," Captain McQuade said after he looked at his pocket watch. "We've got a train to meet. If you finish what you're doing alive, come over to Caborca and ask for Hector Veragua. He can always tell you how to get in touch with me. Any time you want that job."

"Thank you Captain."

"Well I've got to gather my children and be on my way. Why don't you buy yourself another drink? You may as well, while your money's still some good to you." Captain

McQuade shook his head and strode to the door. *"Vámanos, muchachos,"* he said in a ringing cavalryman's voice, and banged out followed by his hulking warriors.

Boag heard the horses mill around while their riders got mounted, and then there was the call of Captain McQuade's command-voice and the hoofs drummed away until distance absorbed the sound.

The bartender said, "You wish something more, *Señor?*"

"Nada, grácias." Boag finished his coffee and settled the tab and went outside. The night was sharp with chill. He thought about bedding down for the night but the juices were running in him. He went back inside; the bartender was going around the room blowing out the lamps. Boag said, "Hey amigo, how do I get to Caborca?"

"Through the pass to the south and down the mountain until you find the river. That is the Rio de la Concepción. You go downstream and you will come to a town with many tall palm trees."

He heard the barkeep latch the door behind him. He was tired and his bad leg was bothering him a little. Ought to sleep it out, but the juices were still pumping and he cinched up the sorrel and rode out toward the pass.

chapter four

1

He heard gunfire, a lot of it. From a hilltop that commanded several thousand acres of desert flats he had a long-distance view of people flitting from rock to rock, powder smoke drifting in tufts, a long line of uniformed troops lying along the parapet of a low bluff shooting down into the flitting figures, riderless horses prancing nervously. Evidently a troop of federals had ambushed a rebel column.

Boag didn't hang around to see how it turned out. The federals were setting up a hand-crank Gatling gun on its wheeled cart and when he rode back behind the hill he heard the thing begin to stutter viciously. Not much chance for the rebels there.

Long rays of morning sun slanted across the hills. The racket of battle receded behind Boag; once, a mile or more to the north of him and running parallel with Boag's course, a horseman riding low to the withers raced through the cuts and gullies and finally disappeared into the ridged badlands —a rebel messenger dispatched for help, Boag judged. It wasn't going to do them any good, there wasn't time to bring reinforcements. He gave that outfit back there half an hour to get cut to pieces by the Gatling gun. There wasn't enough cover in the ambush-ground the federals had picked; the federals had set it up with first-class tactical talent.

The old woman back on the Colorado had been right; the regular troops would win this one, there wouldn't be any overthrow of the provincial government. Governor Pesquiera not only had the troops and the money; it was clear he also had the military brains. Boag wondered what kind of suicidal lunacy had persuaded Captain Shelby McQuade to join up with the losing side. Captain McQuade had always been reckless but he'd seldom been stupid. But now he wanted to kick over the pail and he didn't seem to realize the pail was too full; he wasn't going to kick it over, he was going to stub his toe against it.

It took Boag two days to find his way to Caborca town. Distances down here were always endless. The Concepción was as poor an excuse for a river as the Gila; in a lot of places it was only a dry sandy bed with trees on both banks. The river ran underground here and if you had to you could dig down and find it a few feet below the surface. It wasn't worth the trouble if your life didn't depend on it because a yard's depth of loose fine sand was the worst thing in the world to dig a hole in.

Caborca had very tall palms and a big old battered mission church on a square. There were farms around the town, irrigated by ditch water from the river. Boag passed fat women with burdens on their heads and big farm carts with huge wheels made of solid wood. The huts were painted different pale colors. He bought food for his pack and grain for the horse and moved right on down the river after no more than twenty minutes in the town.

Halfway through the following morning he found Almada's hacienda. The *patron* was a suspicious man but courteous; he accepted Captain McQuade's introduction and said in a curt candid way that he had heard of Mr. Pickett but had never had dealings with the man. He said it in a way that persuaded Boag it was true. Almada didn't know where

Boag might look unless it was farther to the southeast in the mountain country where there were half a dozen aristocratic manor-lords who had fallen on hard times and had taken to trading with bandits for a livelihood. Almada gave Boag two names, Felix Cielo and Don Pablo Ortiz, and showed Boag the door.

2

Two days out of Caborca on his way into the mountains he passed a troop of *rurales,* provincial dragoons on horseback dragging two little twelve-pound brass cannons on horsecarts. Boag swung wide around them because he was familiar with the tedious suspicions of *rurale* officers and in the old days riding dispatch during the campaigns he'd sometimes had to spend hours with them establishing credentials. Now he had no credentials and didn't care to get shot for sport so he cut across behind them and went higher into the timber.

The air got cooler as he climbed into the pines. Here and there he passed empty tunnel mouths and discolored piles of tailings where hopeful hardrockers had tried to strike it rich. It was silver country up here but most of the mines, even the paying ones, had been closed down toward the end of the Maximilian reign and had never reopened because the revolutions against the Austrian crown had spawned hungry battalions of bandits who still prowled the Sierra like dogs gone wild, hunting in vicious packs for scraps. It was easier to give birth to a litter of bandits than it was to get rid of them; the big revolutions were finished now but the bandits still rode, and the mines were still closed, and the owners of the mines were dead or poor or living in exile with their relatives like the old woman he'd left in Yuma.

It was a district that didn't like questions, any questions about anything, and didn't like the people who asked them. Boag got strange looks from everyone because he was black, and hard looks from some when he asked how to find Felix Cielo and Don Pablo Ortiz; it took a long time and almost led to two shootings but in the end he got a *vaquero* drunk enough to direct him to Cielo's place.

It was a fortified *rancho* built back in the days of almost daily Indian raids. It had everything but a moat. The walls of the *hacienda* were five feet thick and slitted with rifle ports; the house was built square around a courtyard and there was a water well in the center of the courtyard so that the Indians couldn't lay siege to the place and kill anyone by thirst.

In that part of the world you measured the age of a town or a *rancho* by the size of its trees. Cielo's establishment was out in the middle of a grass meadow several miles long and almost as wide; the house and its fortified outbuildings sat up on a knoll with command of sixty or seventy square miles of buffalo grass, and the trees around the *hacienda* threw enough shade to make it likely they had been planted by the grandfather of the present *don* even if he himself turned out to be a very old man.

There weren't many cattle in sight, the grass hadn't been grazed, and Boag saw only two men when he approached the house, both on horseback. They looked less like working *vaqueros* than like hardcase bodyguards. They converged toward the gateposts so that they had Boag bracketed between them when he arrived. They both had paired revolvers in crossbelted holsters, *bandoleros* across their shoulders and long rifles across the wide flat wooden horns of their saddles. The rifles weren't exactly pointed at Boag.

He said he wished to see the *don;* he said he had been directed here by Almada of Caborca; he kept both hands empty on the pommel. He said it was a matter of business, there was gold bullion involved. He said he thought the *don* might be interested.

They didn't say much of anything. They took him up to the house and one of them went inside. The other one kept his eyes on Boag and his rifle handy and managed to express the idea that he didn't think it would be a very hard job to put a bullet through the third button of Boag's shirt. Boag dismounted and stood in the shade because it was getting on for the noon hour and the sun was pretty damn hot even at this altitude.

Felix Cielo turned out to be not such a very old man but he might as well have been. He was what remained of an aristocratic horseman, now gone to seed. A thousand gallons of tequila showed in the red veins of his oversized nose. His hands were puffy and his big gut that hung out over his fancy leather belt was not concealed by the intricate woven vest he wore over his stained white shirt. He was somewhere on the sour side of forty and had the eyes of a man who had been kicked more than once and expected to be kicked again. Probably he was drinking up the last of his family fortune and making cheap deals with bandits to postpone bankruptcy.

Boag knew before he started talking that this wasn't the kind of man Mr. Pickett would deal with. He cut it short, asked his questions and got his negative answers and in the end asked where he might look for Don Pablo Ortiz.

3

The wagon road trickled down into the valley. There was an old mine off the side of the road, slag piles and grey buildings and two tunnels that he could see, rusty railroad tracks coming out of both of them to abutments where the ore carts would be dumped. A rusty tilt cart on one of them. This wasn't a mine that had been closed down out of fear; it was a place that was all used up, played out. The earth had been stripped of its goods and the mine had died an honest death.

That down yonder on the plain must be Don Pablo Ortiz's outfit. It was bigger than the Cielo *hacienda* but it shared a lot of its qualities: the adobe Moorish shape, the location on a low knoll surrounded by open flats where you could see your attackers long before they got in shooting range, the fortress sense of the layout, and the quality of decay: there were no big crews of *vaqueros* out herding cattle and there were no cows to herd and the grass had not been eaten.

A windmill sprouted from the central courtyard of the house, looming tall above the place on its rickety wooden trestlework. There weren't any big trees; the place was probably as old as Cielo's but either someone had cut all the trees down for better visibility or no one had ever planted any. There were abundant oleanders ten feet high and even an orchard of pruned low apple trees beside one of the barns; there was plenty of greenery but none of it was high or thick. The *dons* here had wanted nothing that would interrupt their field of fire.

It was an impressive estate and it got more impressive as he approached. You came up at it from below; the knoll was higher than it had looked from the mountains. The *hacienda* lofted itself against the sky like a cliff. It wasn't forbidding, it was imposing; it looked like the kind of mansion you would like to live in after you got very rich. From its eminence it commanded the world beneath it.

It threw long shadows; Boag had ridden more than forty miles since sunup to get here and it wasn't far to nightfall. He reached the barn and rode up past the apple trees and wondered why nobody with a gun had come out to greet him; obviously they had watched him approach, he'd been in plain sight for an hour crossing the grass flats.

There was a semicircle of driveway up to the big oak gate cut into the *hacienda's* front wall; there were twenty posts with iron rings in them for the convenience of guests. He tethered the horse to one of them and walked up to the oak gate. It was twelve or fourteen feet wide and at least ten feet tall, cut into halves like the doors of some great church. A small door was cut into one of the gates. Boag lifted the huge brass knocker and the small door opened before he could clap it.

The man was a very old *vaquero* with a pinfire revolver in his sash. He wore the kind of leather cuffs cattlemen wore to prevent rope-burns.

"Yes?"

"I wish to see the *patrón.*"

The old *vaquero* was uncertain. This was no gunslick bodyguard, Boag observed. An old retainer who'd spent forty years in the saddle chousing cows.

"Cómo se llama?"

"I am called Boag. It is about gold bullion."

The old *vaquero* hadn't made any moves toward the pinfire in his sash. He just stood aside and let Boag walk into the courtyard. The wooden lattice of the windmill dominated the square; a second-story veranda ran around all four sides of it and in two of the corners there were steps going up. The veranda formed a covered gallery for the entrances to all the downstairs rooms; it was typically the kind of house where there was no connecting passage from room to room and you had to come out into the courtyard and down to the next doorway if you wanted to go from one room to another.

There was a profusion of carefully tended flowers in pots and boxes in the courtyard; a great deal of brilliant color and bees rushing around them.

A young woman was coming down the stairs; Boag picked up the movement in the corner of his vision and wheeled and saw her reach the ground and come toward him smiling. It was a blinding smile on a stunning face. She had a cocked ten-gauge shotgun in her arms and it was aimed dead-center on Boag.

Boag froze bolt still.

Behind him the old *vaquero* spoke. "He wishes to see the *patrón* about a matter of gold bullion." Very dry.

"Gold bullion," the young woman echoed. She had a smoky voice. Her eyes stayed on Boag when she spoke to the old *vaquero.* "Did he give a name?"

"I have forgotten it, *Señora.*"

"It's Boag."

"Boag?"

"My name."

"What does this mean, this Boag?"

"Just means Boag."

"You speak with a gringo's accent."

"I come from north of the Border."

"And you wish to see my husband about gold bullion."

"I only want to ask him something. You could point that thing somewhere else."

"You are nervous?" A pink tongue flicked across her lips; she was amused. "The *señora* knows how to use a shotgun, *Señor* Boag, and how not to. Let's make a bargain—you hang your gunbelt on the windmill strut and I shall put down the shotgun and we shall both go and see my husband. You agree?"

"Seguro que sí."

"Very good," she said and Boag hung the forty-five up and followed her up the stairs. She had handed the shotgun to the old *vaquero* and he followed them upstairs; it wasn't quite the bargain Boag had had in mind but if they'd wanted to shoot him they'd have done it by now.

Suddenly he realized the *señora* had stopped on the veranda. She was very still, looking at him, not blinking.

Boag's eyes rested on the pulsing hollow at the base of her throat. Then they slipped down and he caught himself staring at the downed cleft between her breasts. She wore a sunbonnet and a man's shirt open to the third button and a pair of black riding breeches; she was a tall woman with smooth dark skin and proud quivery breasts and a good flare to haunch and rump; and there was vibrant provocation in the way she was looking at him. There was a secret amusement of some kind, and a bold speculation. More like the eye of a girl at a whorehouse bar than an aristocrat's wife.

"Miguel you may see to your duties."

"Sí, Señora."

She turned to a door, passing Boag with a slow flirt of the shoulder. She opened it and spoke into the dimness:

"*Querido.* We have a visitor who wishes to discuss gold bullion with us."

Laughter rang from the darkness within.

4

Don Pablo Ortiz laughed so hard he brought on a fit of coughing which he concealed behind a fragile handkerchief. The *señora* pushed the door shut behind her and Boag tried to get a better look at the man's face but he was just going to have to wait for his eyes to adjust to the bad light. A fish-oil lamp burned on the table beside Don Pablo's chair but it didn't give much light.

The room smelled stale, as if its air hadn't moved in a long time.

"Gold bullion," Don Pablo said again, and chuckled. "Yes, well tell us about this gold bullion, *Señor.*"

"His name is Boag."

"Boag?"

"Just so. Or so he says."

Boag said, "There is a man called Mr. Jed Pickett."

"Ah yes," Don Pablo murmured. "So there is. So there certainly is."

Boag could make him out now. A thin young man gone to waste, the white gentleman's shirt lying wearily against washboard ribs. The pale skin of the Spaniard, a full head of hair that was shot thick with grey and tangled very fine as if he hadn't bothered to comb it in days. Deep brackets of sickness creased his face on both sides of the pale lips; Don Pablo's eyes were dull as slate.

Boag said, "I am looking to find him."

Don Pablo looked him over and burst into laughter again. It doubled him over coughing.

Boag glanced at the *señora.* There was anguish in her eyes but she did not stir.

Don Pablo straightened in his chair, with effort. "*Querida,* a little drink for us all, *por favor.*"

Boag watched her move across the room. When she brought glasses to the table beside her husband he rested a proprietary hand on her rump, a casual and natural intimate gesture; and the *señora* who was no young child of the woods made as if to smile, trying to hide the pain in it. Boag wanted to leave this house of death as fast as he could.

The whiskey moved like a soft warm hand over the saddle-worn muscles of his body. He looked around the big room and thought it bare; there were only a few pieces of furniture, the massive divans and chairs; there were no ornaments on the mantelpiece over the great fireplace and he saw discolored rectangles on two walls as if paintings had hung there but had been removed.

Don Pablo smacked his thin lips. "It is good. Even the dying have a few pleasures, *no es verdad?*"

It was consumption of course. It wasn't the first time Boag had seen it.

The *señora* said, "Are you chilled?"

"You might make a fire now, *querida.*"

A slantwise look at Boag, and she went out of the room; he couldn't read the meaning of her glances.

Don Pablo said, "Now this gold bullion. What has it to do with you?"

"Some of it was mine. A little piece of it."

"And you came all this way trying to get it back."

"Well it seemed like a good idea at the time."

"Have you ever seen a small dog chase a herd of horses around a corral, *Señor* Boag? Did you ever stop to wonder what might happen if the horses decided to stop and let the small dog catch them?"

It gave Boag a very graphic picture of a small mutt being trampled to death by iron-shod hoofs. He smiled over the rim of his glass.

Don Pablo said, "Mr. Jed Pickett has something of mine as well. You and I have that in common." And broke off to cough into his lace.

The *señora* entered with an armload of wood and kindling. She built a fire quickly and well. When the flame caught at the edges she stood up. "It is time for your soup." The eyes came at Boag: "Will you take dinner with us?"

"*Grácias.*"

"I shall bring it up here then."

Don Pablo's shoulders moved. "I can still walk to the dining room."

"You should conserve your strength."

"For dying? No, I can still eat at the table where my father and his father ate."

She rested a hand against the mantel. "Pablo . . . ."

"Querida, ténga la bondad."

She left the room without further protest. The door clicked shut. Don Pablo said, "I am not fit to hold her stirrup."

"Why?"

"It is tiresome looking after a dying man. She could have left me and gone to Mexico City where she comes from. It is not as if she would lose anything by that; I have no one else to leave my estate to, and in any case there is no estate left for her to inherit. She knows all this, and there is no tradition in her background that would make her loyal. But she stays."

"She loves you."

"That would be more than I bargained for with her."

"Sometimes a man gets lucky."

Don Pablo grinned. "You are very wry, *Señor* Boag."

"No. I reckon there are worse things than dying."

"You mean having no one to care about you. Well I suppose that is a point. She worked in a house, you know. One of the best parlors in Mexico City. I would not have taken her out of that except that after a while I could no longer stand the idea of sharing her with other men. She came with me because of course it was a great advancement for her. Nothing was said about love."

"It doesn't always have to be said."

"Of course I was not sick then." Don Pablo began dry-washing his clasped hands.

"About Mr. Pickett," Boag said gently.

"You would like to find him." Don Pablo nodded his head as if to confirm something. "Yes. Well so would I, *Señor.* If it is my last act on earth I should like very much to find Mr. Jed Pickett and have his entrails for guitar strings."

"I thought maybe you might have bought the gold from him."

"I did."

"But?"

"Even a dying man hates to look a fool, *Señor* Boag. I am reluctant to admit the truth to you. I shall do it, but allow me to explain things. An hour will make no difference to you."

"Go ahead then."

Don Pablo coughed and sipped his drink and began to make his explanation. It covered a great deal of ground; it was a tedious apology which did not explain at all, it only tried to excuse. It did not explain, for instance, why Don Pablo insisted on informing a stranger—a black stranger at that—of the fact that his wife had once been a whore in Mexico City. It only ticked off incidents: revolutions, bandits, the mines petering out, the death of the wise uncle who had managed these estates until his death four years ago from the same malaise that now infected the young Pablo.

Boag didn't dislike him but it was hard to find sympathy for him; Don Pablo had too much sympathy for himself, he didn't leave room for anyone else's.

He had contacts in Mexico City, he explained—companions from the days, only a few years ago, when he had been a flippant young blade touring the fandango spots of the city. These contacts knew his good family name and trusted him, or else they were too jaded and cynical to care: in any case they were eager to buy what Don Pablo offered for sale, at a price—the stolen items he traded with the mountain bandits and rebels.

He had dealt a few times with Mr. Jed Pickett in treasures the Pickett gang had collected in its raids on Apache camps in the Sierra Madre: treasures the Apaches in turn had stolen from ranches they raided along both sides of the Border.

Four months ago Mr. Pickett had first mentioned the gold bullion. Don Pablo never knew where it came from; he never asked. A tentative price was settled between them, a price by the ounce because Mr. Pickett was not certain how much gold would be involved. The proposition excited Don Pablo because it meant he could cancel all his debts at once and, he said, "Also it would make a little dowry for Dorotea."

"Your daughter?"

"I refer to the *señora.*"

A dowry for his wife? It was a phrase that made no sense.

Don Pablo said, "I had to strip myself of what few possessions remained, to raise the cash. Our estimate was on the basis of two million pesos. Much of this I had to borrow of course. I signed notes against my estates to do that—mortgages."

Boag didn't need to hear the rest of it because he had already guessed.

Don Pablo wheezed into his handkerchief. "When he came here one week ago he had only three companions and one pack mule and I thought the thing had gone bad, but he was in wickedly high spirits. Over the next thirty-six hours his men trickled into this valley from all directions. They all had pack animals. I gathered not a single pack had been lost. The gold was as he had said it would be, a few pounds less than the maximum I had been prepared to pay for. We weighed the gold on my cattle scales and I counted out one million, nine hundred thousand pesos on this table right here. Most of it was in Mexico City scrip, in denominations of one thousand pesos. It was very easy to carry when you compare it with the bullion. It disappeared into the pockets of himself and his men, and you hardly noticed the bulges."

Boag was impatient. "And then?"

"I am sure you have guessed by now. They leveled their guns at us and backed away to their horses. They took with them not only the nearly two million pesos in cash which I had paid for the gold. They took also the gold."

5

"You are going to say I was a champion of a fool to trust them."

"It crossed my mind," Boag said.

"I did not trust them. My *vaqueros* were armed and watchful. But *vaqueros* are not a match for men like his. They were taken by surprise, overwhelmed before they knew it. Four of my people were killed and three others are still under treatment with the doctor in the town of Coronado."

"You do any damage to the other side?"

"I think two or three of Pickett's *ladrónes* were injured. I saw one whose arm flopped very loosely, I am sure it had been broken by a bullet above the elbow."

"But they took the cash and the gold bullion both."

"Yes."

"Any idea where they went from here?"

"It is a large world, *Señor.*"

"Then Mr. Pickett didn't drop any hints."

"No, he is too clever for that."

"Which way did they ride out?"

"To the south. It means nothing of course."

"Maybe," Boag said.

"You have an idea?"

"How much is that gold really worth, in pesos?"

"You mean if it were clean, if it could be sold in the open market without fear of discovery?"

"Yes."

"Approximately three and one half million pesos."

Boag said, "So Mr. Pickett has more than five million pesos to spend. You could almost buy this whole province for that."

"Well hardly, *Señor.* But it is an impressive sum." Don Pablo's pale hands came together in a prayer clasp. "You said some part of the gold was yours?"

"Yes." Boag refused to be drawn. He was thinking, if I had all that money where would I take it? But it was hard to think like Mr. Jed Pickett. He didn't have the background for it.

He said, "He left about a week ago?"

"Today is Monday. They left here Wednesday evening. It is five days."

"You didn't send anybody after them?"

"I had no one left to send," Don Pablo murmured. He roused himself, shaking his head as though to clear it. "I was obligated to inform my men that I had nothing left with which to pay them, that my estate was under mortgage which could not be repaid, and would be taken from me in due course. I gave them what little I could and dismissed them. The aged one, Miguel, chose to remain with us without pay. He is the only one."

Well it wasn't the way Boag would have done it. At least you could give them a choice. *If you want to get paid you have to go after the son of a bitch and get my money back for me.* But that wasn't realistic, was it; not when you were talking about Mr. Pickett's rawhiders. They had been fighting Yankees and Apaches and Mexicans for twenty-odd years while Don Pablo's *vaqueros* had been chousing cows.

Miguel appeared. *"La comida."* Miguel helped Don Pablo out of the chair and half carried him. Boag trailed them down the stairs and across the courtyard in the dusk. There was the rasp of cicadas, a cool dry wind, light clouds scudding by.

You could see where there had been paintings and candelabra in the dining room; now there was only the table and a few chairs which probably had been brought up from crew's quarters. *Señora* Dorotea served the meal on chipped Indian pottery plates; the Don ate soup while the rest of them ate the meat of a rabbit Miguel had shot. The cattle herds, it was explained, had been sold along with everything else to raise money to pay for Mr. Pickett's gold. It had been Don Pablo's plan to sell the estate to the men in Monterrey and Durango who held the mortgages; then he would have been able to take Dorotea to a mountain resort for the cure. The cure seldom worked but it was worth the attempt; what else was there? There would have been money enough to buy their own resort.

"Now it is all ashes," Don Pablo whispered into his soup.

It was as if he was already dead; it was just taking him

some time to quit breathing. Boag said, "How long do they give you?"

There was a sharp glance from Miguel. The *señora* did not look up. Don Pablo said, "A few months, perhaps a year, perhaps two years or five. No one knows, really."

"Then maybe you're giving up a little early."

Don Pablo cackled. It made him cough.

6

He lay on a straw tick in a small room off the veranda.

A light rapping at the door; he looked up and it was the *Señora* Dorotea. She rested her shoulder against the doorframe. "I was lonely," she said.

He looked into her eyes; she gave a little smile as if to say she knew what had not been said and was not going to be said.

When he touched her cheek he felt her tremble. He ran his fingertips up into her thick dark hair, surprised by the cool smoothness of her skin. Her woman-smell filled him.

She sat on the cot beside him; the heavy rope of her hair swung forward. She bent down and he tasted her mouth and then she slipped her face away to guide his lips down her throat.

They took a long time making love.

Then he lay on his back, belly rising and falling with his breath, and she laid her head back against the hard muscles of his thigh and spoke in a voice drowsy with spent passion: "I think we have both been too long without this."

She turned and curled up with her fists together against him, one knee hooked over his body. He ruffled her hair. "I feel hound-dog lazy."

"Were you a slave?"

"When I was a little kid."

"So was I. In a way."

He turned his head to look at her. She said, "Pablo has not bought me and he does not own me. He knows that."

"I thought you were married to him."

"I am. But he has told me I may leave when I wish."

"But you've stayed."

"He needs looking after."

"You're a good woman."

"I think I am," she said. "When I said I was a slave I meant before, when I was a girl in the city. I was bought and put into a house there."

"He told me about that."

"Did he also tell you he bought me from the madam?"

"He didn't say that."

"But I had a choice. I could have run away from him. I knew he wouldn't try very hard to get me back. Not that he did not want me, but he has never forced me to do anything unless it was what I wished."

"He loves you."

"He has never said that," she said, and it made Boag remember the same conversation with Don Pablo.

"This gold," she said. "Do you really expect to take any of it away from that man?"

"Well I expect to try."

"Is it enough to die for?"

"He owes me something else besides gold. There was a friend of mine. . . ." But he didn't go on about Wilstach; it would probably make no sense to her. "He needs killing."

"But how will you fight him if you find him?"

"Dirty."

Her head stirred. Boag said, "There's no difference between one way of fighting and another. The winner is the man still alive afterward."

"If we could help, Don Pablo and I . . . ."

"Yes?"

". . . Do you think you could try to recover Pablo's money as well?"

Well there had to be a reason, he supposed bleakly.

She read his mind; she sat up. "That is not the reason I came to you tonight. Did you think it was?"

He made no answer of any kind; his silence argued with her, however, and in the end she got off the cot and reached for her clothes. "I suppose it is what you must believe. I was foolish, I should have said nothing."

"All right. Forget it."

"I shall try to. I hope you will also."

He reached for her. "Come on then, let's do this again." In relief he laughed till his stomach hurt. And when they had made love he kissed her thoroughly on the mouth. "That's to be sure you won't forget me right away."

She teased him. "I have a very poor memory."

He kissed her again.

He had been a soldier all the years; in the Army you learned not to think about women except when there were women within reach. Either you had women or you did not, and if you did not have them there was nothing but pain in thinking about them. But he knew he was going to think about Dorotea. They had not had much time together but it was enough to make him wish there was more.

There was nothing dog-in-the-manger about Don Pablo Ortiz. He summoned Boag to his chambers in the early morning and when Miguel had left the room the young Don said, "Are you a man of means, *Señor* Boag?"

"Do I look it?"

"You look like a penniless black gringo to me. But I have learned something about appearances."

"I am what I look like."

"And you seek to do battle single-handed against a cutthroat army. It would not be putting it too strongly to state that you have the life expectancy of a lit sulphur match."

"I'd rather not put it just like that."

"Do you know what I think, *Señor?* I think you are hoping you never find Jed Pickett. You are hoping you will continue to arrive at places to find that Jed Pickett is no longer there, he is still a week ahead of you. He will always be a week ahead of you, Boag; I think he was born a week ahead of you."

"If I don't really want to catch him why should I keep chasing him?"

"I think it gives you something to do, something to justify your existence. And I think you hate being afraid. You hate it that much."

Boag thought, it was true. Not once in his life had he been so afraid as that night in the river in the swirling afterwash of the *Uncle Sam*'s paddlewheels, the water tumbling him over and over until he was sure he would drown, and knowing that if he surfaced the guns on deck would finish him. Mr. Jed Pickett had no right doing that to a man.

"So you have to prove something now," Don Pablo said in his voice that was half a wheeze. "You will of course get killed and that will be the proof that you were not afraid. The only one who will know it is a lie is yourself, and of course when you are dead no one can force you to confess it."

"You're a little deep for me now."

"*Señor* Boag, I have seen the eyes you exchange with Dorotea."

Boag stiffened.

Don Pablo waggled his frail hand. "Did she visit you in the night? I suppose it does not matter. I will be truthful. If you were a man who could afford to buy a villa like this one then I should not object to anything you did; I would be pleased to see Dorotea go with a man who can make her happy. I suspect if you asked her to ride away with you this morning she would do it without a backward look."

"You're wrong."

"No."

"Shall we ask her?" Boag said in the most formal Spanish he knew. He got up to move toward the door.

"Wait. Hear me out."

"Get it said, then."

"I have accustomed her to a certain kind of life. I can no longer provide it myself. But when I look into your future I must ask you to get on your horse and go. For Dorotea's sake, *no es verdad?*"

Boag studied the ravaged face. "That was what I aimed to do anyway. But after I go you ask her. The trouble with both of you, you don't trust each other enough."

"You are very kind," Don Pablo wheezed. "I hope we meet again."

When Boag rode away she was standing just outside the gate and she was still watching him, one arm raised to shade her eyes. When he had his last look at her from a low hill four miles out, she was only a speck.

chapter five

1

After that it was days and days on horseback, going from town to town trying to ask questions without being shot for it.

It took a week to get a line on Mr. Pickett. Along the Rio Bavispe in a town called Huásabas there was a fat man in a *cantina* who knew Mr. Pickett by sight from the old scalp-bounty days and said he had seen Mr. Pickett ride through the town two weeks ago with six hardcase riders and several pack animals. So they had split the bunch up again. Heading for where?

The fat man said Mr. Pickett had headed out up the mountain toward Granados, but in that town Boag found no trace of the rawhiders. He cast around for spoor in the memories of goatherds and *vaqueros* and mountain people of indeterminate occupation; it took another four days before he turned up a trace of Mr. Pickett's passage at Mazatán, west of the Yaqui River. Again Mr. Pickett had been seen riding away to the south; this time it was said he had nine tough men with him and at least half a dozen pack mules. For rawhiders with a lot of spending money they had been curiously well behaved, they hadn't treed the town the way gringo gangs liked to do. Possibly Mr. Pickett had given orders to be on good behavior because that way nobody would notice them, but it was having the opposite effect because the town had noticed how well behaved these toughs were.

The trail was not getting any warmer but Boag was patient. He had nothing else to do.

It was getting on for the middle of May; along the Yaqui River the heat was intense. Boag's sorrel wore out and he had to give ten Yankee dollars along with it in trade for a sturdy blue roan mare. He was nearly down to the twenty dollars he had started with before he'd rolled the poker player in Yuma.

Here and there he passed the signs of combat and the tracks of wheeled cannon carts. Rebels and troops were having it out but the warfare in the countryside didn't seem to have much effect on the villagers Boag talked to; perhaps they had lived with revolutions so long they had got bored with them.

In Nuri there was a mescal-swilling *alcalde* who was glad to have a stranger to drink with; the *alcalde* was a gossip and a philosopher. From three hours of his talk Boag gleaned a few shavings. Fourteen horsemen, leading nine pack mules, had passed through the area more than two weeks earlier; no one had recognized any of them but it was thought probable that they had to do with the revolution, so no one approached them.

"Which side?"

"Who knows," said the *alcalde* in his cups. "Does it matter?"

The riders and pack animals had moved on to the west, back toward the Yaqui River.

Boag went that way. But it was not until four days later in Cocorit that he found traces of them again. A talkative bartender in the *cantina* on the central square. "Yes there were fourteen men, I counted them because I was concerned about how many bullet holes there might be after they left. But they behaved themselves with distinction. They were here the one night, very courteous to everyone but they kept mainly to themselves. In the morning they traded a few horses with the stable man, Cruz, and they left."

"Their leader," Boag said. "A man with a yellow mustache and pits in the skin of his face? Not a very big man?"

"No, I do not recall him that way at all, *Señor*. The leader was a very large man in fact."

Boag thought about that. "A lot of brown hair on the backs of his hands?"

"Exactly, *Señor,* that is the man."

Ben Stryker, the *segundo*.

But where did that put Mr. Pickett? If he wasn't traveling with his men, where was he?

Anyhow there were at least six or seven men missing. There had been twenty or more of them at first; now the reports were fairly consistent, thirteen or fourteen men at most.

So Mr. Pickett was off somewhere else with half a dozen men. Doing what?

It looked as if Boag was following the wrong bunch. But it was the only trail he had to follow.

Cruz at the livery barn was a nervous little chatterbox who chewed on coco leaf while he talked. Yes he still had three of the horses the gringos had traded; they were in the corral, would the *señor* like him to point them out?

Boag didn't know why he bothered to look. He'd never seen their horses before anyway. They'd had a remuda of fresh mounts ready for them on the Gila River where they'd beached the Uncle Sam under the trees. He hadn't ever set eyes on those horses so it wasn't surprising that none of the mounts in Cruz's corral looked familiar.

It was just that it helped give him the feeling he still had some kind of contact with them. The thread was frayed but it was still a thread.

"Was there among them a man with a yellow mustache and a pitted face?"

Cruz did not recall such a man although of course there were a dozen men or more and it was many weeks ago and he could not remember faces all that clearly. "But the leader was a striking man, striking, a very tall man, he spoke Spanish very well but with a Yankee drawl, his accent was not so good as yours, *Señor*."

"How many horses did you sell them?"

"Five, it was all I had to spare."

"Any of them have distinctive markings?"

Cruz had to think about it, visibly. Boag found a silver peso in his Levi's and placed it on the flat-sawed top of a corral post. Cruz covered it with his hand. "There was one sorrel with a very pale mane and tail, I recall. Almost like a palomino's mane and tail, yet the horse itself was very dark red or brown."

"Any of them have a split shoe, anything like that?"

"You mean something that would leave a hoofprint you could recognize. No, *Señor,* I recall nothing like that."

"The brand on this horse with the palomino's mane?"

"That was a horse from Chihuahua, *Señor,* it had several brands and I believe the most recent was the big circle of the Ochoa *rancho.*"

When Boag rode out of the place Cruz's voice followed him: "I hope you find your friends."

2

Then he lost the spoor for more than a week. No one to the south or west had seen the gang. It was farm country getting down toward the Gulf; there were plenty of people, too many for the rawhiders to have passed unseen. So they must have doubled back. Boag rode back to Nuri and singled out the *alcalde* who liked to drink.

"It is good to see you again, *Señor* Boag."

"Let me buy you a mescal, *alcalde.*"

"*Simpático.* Like your friend the tall gringo."

"He bought you a drink too, did he?"

"Only four days ago it was."

Boag grinned to hide his excitement. "So they did come back this way."

"Nine of them did. With their pack mules." The *alcalde* lifted his mescal in toast. *"Salud y amor, Señor* Boag. I think your friend was very glad to hear you were looking for him."

"You told him about me."

"Yes of course. He said it had been a long time since he had seen you and he looked forward with keen pleasure to seeing you again."

"I don't suppose he told you where that might be."

"Well he did say if you should return I could tell you he was going to spend a few days in San Ignacio. He hopes you will find him there before he has to leave."

"I'll just bet he does," Boag said.

3

So Ben Stryker's bunch knew Boag was behind them. Knew his name, from the *alcalde.* He wondered what they thought about that. It had to worry them a little. But he wished he hadn't told the *alcalde* his name because if Stryker had known only that a black man was looking for him it would have been more mysterious.

San Ignacio was a foothill village well to the east of the Yaqui River. It was a hot place built on the south slope of a barren hill; a stupid place to build a town. There were 'dobe huts with thatched roofs scattered around the hillside with dirt paths worn from one 'dobe to the next but there was nothing regular enough to be called a street. Even the church looked poor.

Boag reconnoitered from a distance. He rode all the way around the village and then approached it from the upper end. He supposed he was looking for a dark horse with palomino mane and tail; he didn't see one. He only saw two horses at all. One was tethered to a picket rope behind somebody's hut. The other had a saddle on it and was tied to the hitching rail in front of a building that probably served as *cantina* and general store and post office and whatever else the town had need of.

His anticipation had cooled by now. He didn't see any place in this village where you could hide fifteen horses and mules. Of course it was possible they had put a couple of animals in each hut and paid the villagers to keep silent. But that seemed an awful lot of preparation to go through if they knew there was only one man looking for them and they couldn't even be sure he would ever come this way.

More likely they'd leave one man here to see about Boag. That would be the horse hitched in front of the *cantina.* It had a Mexican saddle but that didn't mean anything, Mr. Pickett's men had been in Mexico off and on for years and of course some of them like Gutierrez were Mexicans themselves.

He kind of hoped it would be Gutierrez. He wanted to meet up with Gutierrez again.

He had no patience to wait for nightfall, which perhaps would have been the wiser thing to do because in daylight there was no way at all to approach the *cantina* without being seen from inside it.

He sized up the *cantina's* openings. There were windows on all four sides, but not many of them and not large ones; in these hot places you didn't build in a whole lot of windows for the sun to beat on. The front of the place actually offered the best approach; there was only one window, set high in the wall to the right of the door. The door was shut against the heat and it didn't seem to have any openings in it big enough to sight a gun through.

Boag dismounted fifty yards from the *cantina* and approached from an angle that kept the saddled horse at the hitch rail between him and that window. They could see him coming but they couldn't get a clear shot.

With his shoulders braced stiff against a half-expected bullet he entered what might have been the town square if it had been more regular and had more buildings. His eyes flicked all the corners in sight, the huts and the church and the *cantina.*

A woman in a loose frayed dress walked slowly across toward one hut, supporting her pregnant abdomen in both hands. A dog lay asprawl and panted in the strip of shade beside the church.

The feel of the place was wrong; demons were on the prowl. Boag stopped sixty feet from the saddled horse and turned a slow circle on his heels.

The church door opened and a soldier came out onto the top step. A Mexican infantryman with a .45-90 rolling-block rifle. It was held across his chest at the port-arms position. The soldier just stood there, he didn't make a move.

The pregnant woman stepped aside to let another soldier walk out of the hut she was bound for. She curled past the soldier and went inside. The soldier also held his rifle at port-arms and watched Boag with weary indifference.

Soldiers stepped out of all the huts around the ragged square.

In the end a Lieutenant of Infantry emerged from the *cantina* with a corporal behind his left shoulder. The Lieutenant's holster flap was unbuttoned, but he didn't bother reaching for the revolver. "You will abandon your gunbelt please, *Señor* Boag."

"What the hell for?"

"You are under arrest by authority of Governor Ignacio Pesquiera."

"For what?"

"I was not told the charges," the Lieutenant said. He gestured wide to encompass the eight soldiers and their rifles. "Do you care to fight the drop, *Señor?*"

Boag looked around at them all. He'd been so long in the Cavalry he hadn't even thought about Infantry. Not everybody had a horse.

It was pretty elaborate just to put the grab on one man. A Lieutenant and a detail of soldiers—*rurales,* they were, militia of Sonora.

Well if they had wanted to kill him they'd have done it. They wanted to talk to him. He would find out what it was all about.

Boag dropped the gunbelt in the dirt.

4

Laced with hurts he lay in the jail at Ures and in spite of the crowded stench of it the warmth and the pain enveloped him and sleep rolled his head against the wall.

It had been two days' march down from San Ignacio and in Ures they had thrown him into jail without explanation. He kept waiting for someone to come and question him or accuse him of something but for four days they had done nothing except feed him slop twice a day. From that or from the water he had got dysentery, for which one of the guards had prepared a concoction which he dished out to everyone on alternate mornings; it was the old remedy of bones burnt to ashes and it worked well enough to keep you from losing your mind. But that left Boag more free to hate.

It was a helpless anger. No one told him why he was here. On the fourth day he began to rage around the jail because at least it would make them pay attention to him and perhaps that would cause them to tell him something useful. But they only worked him over with pistol-butts and riding quirts.

Like most Mexican jails it was not divided into cells. It was a big cavernous room which no one had cleaned in years. The filth was overpowering. There were chamberpots but not enough of them. Men with dysentery occupied them, squatting for half-hour stretches in twisted agony while other men could no longer wait their turns and defecated on the floor.

Boag spent hours considering how he might tear something apart that he could use to pry the bars open. There was nothing. The place was not all that well built and if he had had a friend on the outside it would have been easy in the night to goad a mule into kicking a hole through the dry adobe wall. The floor was rammed earth and it might be possible to dig out but that would take forever and there were no tools.

On the fourth morning a guard with his back to the barred door had lighted a cigar and accidentally dropped a handful of sulphur matches. He had picked most of them up but two had rolled under the bars and Boag managed to hide them in his socks.

It was the sixth day when two guards took him out and walked him up a corridor into a small dusty room occupied by a middle-aged warrant officer with a drooping black mustache. The two guards stayed with Boag, sat him down in a chair and stood behind his shoulders.

The warrant officer was drinking wine out of a leather sack with a spout on it. "Who are you scouting for, Boag? Who sent you?"

"Nobody sent me. You got any charges against me?"

"Sedition, will that do?"

"What's that supposed to mean?"

"Giving aid and comfort to the rebels."

"What rebels?"

"You were seen talking at considerable length with a gringo mercenary who is known to be in the employ of the rebel bandits."

Captain Shelby McQuade. Boag said, "We used to soldier together. We were talking about old times."

"Of course you were," the warrant officer said, not so much in disbelief as in indifference.

"Do I get a trial?"

"Political trials have been postponed until the revolt is put down."

"That could be years."

"I suppose it could," the warrant officer said and yawned.

"You went to a lot of trouble to arrest me. How come I'm all that important?"

"Any enemy of the government is important to us."

"Come on," Boag said. "I don't give a damn about your politics down here and I think you know that."

"Then tell us who you were scouting for."

"If I do can I go?"

"Perhaps."

"You'll have to do a little better than that."

"Perhaps we'll break one of your fingers and then ask you again."

"You won't find out much. I was scouting for myself. I'm not working for any rebels."

"Would you like some wine, Boag?"

"I wouldn't mind."

"Thirst can be overpoweringly persuasive, we find. I believe we shall lock you up in a private room for a few days without water and see what you have to say after that. You see we are in no hurry." The warrant officer yawned again and waved at the two guards and they took Boag down the corridor and threw him into a cubicle. He heard the key rattle in the lock.

It didn't make a whole lot of sense unless you made an assumption. Assume that Mr. Pickett had the Governor's ear and then it all made sense. Mr. Pickett was having his fun. That was the only way to explain it. Mr. Pickett told his friend the Governor there was a black man annoying him. Because the Governor owed Mr. Pickett a favor he had Boag picked up and they were going to sweat him for a while just for the hell of it. Boag had heard about Governor Ignacio Pesquiera for years: a man who enjoyed inflicting pain.

It had to be something like that because nobody other than Mr. Pickett had any real reason for it. They couldn't possibly believe Boag had any connection with the rebels. Otherwise they would have done what the warrant officer had threatened to do: smash a few of his fingers and indulge in some other tortures until they got the information out of him they thought he carried. And they would have done that right at the outset, they wouldn't have waited a week. So they weren't interested in information, and that meant they knew Boag didn't have any information. It came back to Mr. Pickett.

Mr. Pickett just wanted him out of the way.

When they got tired of playing games they would turn him loose and let him get fifty feet or five miles away and then they'd shoot him down in the back and write it up as another prisoner shot trying to escape.

That friendly *alcalde* back in Nuri was a public official and no doubt owed his job to the Governor.

There was only one satisfaction in it. They'd gone to a lot of trouble to bring him in and that meant he had worried Mr. Pickett, if only a little.

It would be very nice now to get out of this place and disappear for a while and let Mr. Pickett worry some more, knowing Boag was loose somewhere and knowing it could come any time from any direction: a gunshot in the night, a knife through the back ribs, a pair of strong black arms waiting just inside a dark doorway.

It would be very nice but it didn't look likely. It didn't even look possible. This cell had been designed to keep men in. It was getting a little old and dried-out but there was no evident way out of it except through the door and that was made of heavy thick wood with hinges on the far side. There was a tiny window but even if you broke the bars you couldn't squeeze through it. There was no bed, only a raised platform of adobe along one wall with a blanket on it. The chamberpot was made of clay and would break if you sat too hard on it.

He thought about waiting them out but he had seen what thirst did to men in the desert and he knew if he had to suffer that for more than a few days he would go out of his head and would be in no condition to plan escapes after that. There had to be some alternative.

There had to be but probably there wasn't; Mexican prisons were well known for being impossible to get out of.

So this is how it ends, he thought. Dead in a foul Ures jail with nobody to mourn him.

He studied his world with great care for a day and a half but there was nothing to use for a lever.

At noon on the second day his tongue was beginning to swell. He had chipped a pea-sized pebble of adobe off a corner of the sill and that helped a little, keeping it rolling on his tongue, but soon there wouldn't be enough saliva to work any more.

When the guard came to get the chamberpot Boag said, "Can you get me a Bible?"

It was the one thing they were not likely to refuse him. The Bible was brought to him along with the emptied chamberpot and Boag made a show of sitting down to start reading it. When the guard left and the door slammed and the lock clattered, Boag turned the Bible upside down and shook it and hefted it for weight. It might not be enough but it was the only chance he had so he had to try it.

5

If it worked it would work only because the building was so old. The massive wooden door had dried out and shrunk just a little with age, leaving slim gaps along the top and bottom to admit ribbons of lamplight at night, and there were thin cracks between the vertical planks of the door as well.

So there was some air circulation there.

It would have been neater and easier with a knife, but they had taken everything from him, even his belt and belt buckle. So he tore up the blanket with his fingernails and his teeth. He tore it in strips and he kept one strip aside. The rest of them he tore into little pieces of cloth. The blanket was some kind of homespun material, it wasn't wool. Wool would have been no good at all. If the blanket had been wool he would have had to use his own clothes.

It would be best to try it late in the night when there

weren't many people awake in the prison. There would be night guards but not as many of them as during the day. And if he did get out he wanted the night for cover.

It wasn't likely he'd get out. It was likely he'd get killed. In fact he might die of his own trick. But it was better than what they had in mind for him.

He tore the binding off the Bible and removed the pages in clumps and then separated the clumps until he had hundreds of flimsy pages isolated. He crumpled each page in his fist into a loose ball of paper and he piled the paper up against the old door in a big heap. He mixed the small pieces of blanket into the pile and when it was ready, some time around midnight he guessed, he took one of the matches out of his sock and ignited the pyre.

Small flames trickled up from the bottom corners of the heap of paper and suddenly the whole thing crashed into flame. It was a hot roaring bonfire that wouldn't last long at all and he was afraid the wood was too thick to catch. He couldn't stay to make sure; the heat drove him back across the cell with his arm flung up across his face. He coughed in the smoke and climbed onto the platform that passed for a bunk. Held his face twisted into the bars of the little window. The flames sucked a wind through the opening and he was able to breathe here.

The heat was a blast of agony. It was good he hadn't had to rip up his clothes for fuel because without that protection he would have been singed and scorched and blistered from head to foot.

He kept his back hunched against it and pushed his face against the bars. Smoke wheeled into him and burnt his throat and he thought, while he coughed white hot pain, that if this was what Don Pablo Ortiz endured every time he had a coughing spasm then Don Pablo was a braver man than Boag had thought.

The heat pushed at him as though he were in the fire, not ten feet from it. But paper burned very hot while it burned and he had no confidence it would last long enough to ignite the door; the heat began to drop and so did the blinding light of it and when he looked at it the paper heap was collapsing into a small pile of uncurling papers with grey edges.

He pounced across the room and kicked the paper back up against the door and tried to shove some of it under the crack with the toe of his boot.

He did not want to think about what he was doing to the Bible.

Little flames flickered around the lower edge of the door and he kept crowding the ash toward them because there were still fires in the ashes.

The door was burning. Here and there it turned red at the splinters. The flames had caught and it was not burning high like the paper but it was burning, turning black beneath the flames as the fire crept upward along the cracks where air came through from the corridor and fed it.

He watched the last of the Bible disintegrate. Little patches of blanket-cloth still smoldered and he shoved them all under the door. Then he picked up the single strip of blanket he had saved and carried it back to the window with him and stood there in the clean wind, watching the small fires nibble the wood.

Finally he knew he had it licked when he saw flames sliding in through the cracks from the outside of the door. It meant the fire was climbing up the corridor side of the door. The draft would draw the flames through the cracks to this side and that would keep it burning.

He had been parched before. The smoke sucked the last moisture out of him and he almost strangled dry-coughing; he had to swallow a dozen times in panic before the saliva began to run reluctantly in his throat.

He heard them running down the corridor. The boots clattered to a halt outside the burning door and he heard a voice. "Get buckets—get water!"

Then another voice with the timbre of command. "Never mind, let him fry in there."

The first voice: "But the door."

"It will have to be replaced in any case."

Just the two of them, Boag decided; there were no others. Yet.

He judged the door and it had to be now, he had to hope the fire had weakened it enough.

He made his run.

7

He left the floor halfway across the room, launched himself into a flying dropkick and hit the door fairly low, feet first, expecting the tough old timbers to hold firm and break his feet.

But the wood was dry and brittle and the fire had eaten enough of it. He went through in a tangled crashing of broken wood and angry flames.

He skinned his ankle on the corridor floor and rolled fast; it was a blind lunge but it caught somebody across the shins and the man came down on top of Boag. A voice shouted and Boag slithered out from under the flailing body, found the man's head as it lifted; Boag whipped the length of blanket-strip around the man's neck and yanked it tight as a garotte.

He saw the other one back away fumbling for his revolver.

Boag clamped a one-hand grip on the rag that circled his man's throat; he whipped up the guard's revolver with his free hand but he wasn't fast enough and the man on his feet began shooting. One of the bullets slammed into Boag's man. Boag felt the body lurch against him. He fired past the man's ear and saw the other guard flinch from the shooting; Boag pulled trigger again and it scored. The guard went down.

Flames burned strong around the jagged hole in the door, sucking a wind through that moaned in the corridor. Boag batted his prisoner across the temple with the gun, but it wasn't needed, the man had a bullet somewhere in his guts and there was no fight in him. Boag left him, left the blanket-strip, scooped up the other guard's revolver and ran down the hall with revolvers in both fists.

A guard bolted around the far bend into the end of the corridor. Boag snapped a shot that drove the guard back behind cover. *Remember now you've used two from the left hand and one from the right.* Were they the kind who loaded six or were they the kind who loaded five and left the chamber empty under the pin? Assume that; assume you have seven left.

The gunbarrel was poking around the corner and Boag flattened himself in a doorway. The guard down there sprayed the corridor, shooting blind. Boag let him take his five shots and then Boag was out and running again and he heard the guard retreat in panic. He heard empty shell cases clatter on the floor.

He tried doors as he passed them. Three were locked. The fourth stood ajar but it was only an empty cell. Boag reached the corner and triggered a blind shot around it, burst around the corner, guns up, and saw the guard frantically plugging ammunition into his revolver. Boag sighted and fired quickly but not too quickly. The bullet snapped the guard back against the doorframe and he slid to the floor leaving a blood smear on the wood.

How many more of them and where would they come from? Boag tried to remember the route by which they had brought him into the prison. Where were the exits? He stepped across the dying guard, scooping up the man's revolver; he crouched to finish the reloading job and took the guard's ammunition pouch with him back into the dark offices.

He made several turnings, moving without sound now; he

heard voices shouting in the labyrinth behind him. Some fool fired a shot in some other part of the building and the echoes clanged around in the night.

He tried a door slowly and peered through the crack. It was a side door into the room where they had taken his belongings from him. There was a long counter with locked cabinets behind it.

He didn't have time to seek out his things. But he knew where he was now and he slipped into the room, pulled the door shut behind him and loped across to the far door. Beyond it was a corridor and at the far end of that was a courtyard, and across the courtyard was a gate to the street of Ures.

The gate would be shut of course and there were guard towers up on the walls. It would be impossible to cross the courtyard in the open on foot and even if he did, there would still be the gate, at least ten feet high under its arch of adobe.

But maybe the racket would cause enough confusion. He plunged into the corridor and ran the length of it on his toes, and stopped just inside the open archway in the shadows to look out across the cobbled courtyard.

An alarm bell was clanging above him. The moon in its last sliver was just disappearing downhill to the west and there were clouds across the stars; it was good and dark and perhaps that would confuse their aim. But there was still that gate.

The juices were pumping in him. He felt his lips peel back from his teeth in a rictus of a grin.

He heard running boots inside the jail somewhere; he listened with concern but they didn't seem to be drawing closer. Then he heard a drum of hoofbeats.

It was coming from outside—the courtyard or the street?

He put his head out slowly but there was nothing moving in the courtyard except one guard who was coming down the ladder from one of the watch towers, carrying a flaming torch above his head. There were lanterns set into the wall and the guard took his torch toward one of them.

The hoofbeat racket boiled up and Boag saw the horsemen

mill to a halt outside the iron gate. Some yelling was exchanged from the riders to the men on top of the wall. Nobody knew what the alarums were about; there had been shooting inside the jail.

"You'd better let us in then."

Boag heard the grinding of a chain. That would be the mechanism that opened the gate.

The guard with the torch had reached the first lantern and was touching the lantern with the flame when Boag shot him down. The torch rolled away on the cobblestones and the guard crabbed his way back toward the steps, trying to get away from the light that pinned him. The troops were charging into the compound now and Boag waited for them to get close enough; they started to dismount and deploy and that was when Boag started shooting. It drove most of them toward cover and Boag ran out onto the cobblestones, plunging into the rearing confusion of horses before anybody could get a clear shot at him.

He caught a horse by the reins and lifted himself into the saddle. Laid himself flat across it and whacked the horse's flank with a revolver, hard. The horse reared and he saw its wickedly rolling eye; it came down running and he steered it toward the gate. Over the pound of hoofs and the shouts and the gunshots he could hear the winches grinding and he saw the gates swinging; they were trying to close them, to shut him in, but the horse squeezed through and Boag filled his lungs and bellowed:

"By God old Boag made it!"

And then the rifles on top of the wall opened up and he felt something slam into his back. It almost knocked him off the horse.

Christ I've been shot.

He clutched the saddle and kicked the beast frantically. The horse swept him into the alleys of Ures and the shooting behind him stopped, and there was no sound but the clatter of the horse's shoes on the stones and the thunder of blood in Boag's ears while the world began to reel.

In a midnight-dark, midnight-silent street he reined in. He

could feel the moist warm blood along his flank; the bullet had sliced across the lower part of his back on the right side and traveled through part of his thigh before it went out. This was no time to take stock of that; he would worry later about what vital parts might have been hit—or he would die and not have to worry about it.

He had to give them something else to think about.

The store ahead had a porch roof that ran the length of the boardwalk in front of it. Fish-oil lanterns hung under the porch roof. From the saddle he reached out and plucked a lantern off its hook, unscrewed the filler cap and threw the lantern against the wall. The oil splashed out and a little fire started there. He guided the horse ten feet along the boardwalk and picked off another lamp and threw it down too; he went the length of the block throwing lamps on the boardwalk and when he galloped away up the street the porch was starting to burn healthily. Give it five minutes and the whole block would be in flames. It was the dry season and there was a good strong breeze.

His head was getting fuzzy. *Have to get out of this town. I lit enough fires for one night.* He felt the blood running and thought maybe they had put out Boag's fire but he wasn't going to give it up before he had to. He whacked the horse to a canter and clung wildly to the pitching saddle and fled the town of Ures.

chapter six

1

Later he had a hard time sorting out the rest of that night in his memory; it never came together in a piece, there were only isolated instants. Like a night battle seen by the light of its artillery flashes.

Ures lay in the slot of a valley with the slopes of the Sierra Madre on both sides of it. The main road out led down the Rio Sonora to the provincial capital at Hermosillo and then to the Gulf. Boag had enough alertness left in him not to take the main road. He remembered putting the horse up into the mountains. He thought vaguely he was heading east but he wasn't sure and it really made no difference to speak of; he had no destination in mind except escape.

It was Yaqui country, bandit country; not many travelers were fool enough to travel it, especially by night. But there wasn't much they could do to Boag that hadn't already been done.

When he got behind the first rising hill and the lights of town were blotted out by the land mass he stopped the horse and stripped off his shirt and made a ragged sort of binding for his wound. He was suffering from shock, he'd seen it in combat and recognized it in himself; chills and a kind of euphoria and a circling faintness with the blood drifting from his head. What you did for a case like Boag's was lay him down somewhere warm and wrap him up in clean bandages and warm blankets and get hot soup down him and hope he didn't die on you.

For a while he tried to persuade himself that if the bullet had cut any important organs he'd have died by now. It wasn't very convincing; he'd known men shot in the guts or the kidneys who'd lasted a week and then expired.

But Boag only had one thing left and that was the knowledge that he wasn't going to give up.

Later he recalled falling off the horse. It took him somewhere between five minutes and two hours to get back on the saddle. First he had to persuade the unnerved horse to stand still and ignore the smell of fresh blood. Then he had to hitch himself up an inch at a time into the saddle, and every inch drove splinters of red agony through all his fibers, and most of the time he believed he was not going to make it because the muscles just didn't have the strength any more; the body was ready to quit before the head was, but Boag forced the body to obey.

The rest of it was mostly blacked out and never came back to him.

Somewhere in the early morning he had a few moments of awareness. The horse had stopped to drink out of a stream. Sunlight flickered through the pine branches and dappled the stream with dancing pins. The sunrise mist hung above the water and there was dew on the ground. It was a very peaceful scene filled with beauty and Boag thought it was probably the approach to the Pearly Gates, which surprised him a little because he didn't expect they were going to let him in there, especially after setting the Bible on fire.

But then he thought, *Hell I'm a good soldier, I'll stand on my record.* He remembered where he was: he had to get back to the troop and get the news to General Crook's headquarters that Al Sieber had found out where the Geronimo bunch was hiding, the *rancheria* in the Sierra. Now which way was it to Captain Gatewood's camp?

He was falling off the horse when a couple of Tenth Cavalrymen caught him and carried him over into the sunshine and laid him down and threw a blanket across him.

A little later he woke up again and Captain McQuade was looking down into his face. Boag knew it was part of the same dream.

Captain McQuade said, "What the hell, Boag?"

"Captain we got to get word to General Crook. Sieber's got Geronimo located back in there."

"That's all right, Boag, we'll take care of it."

"Thank you, Captain."

Captain McQuade was talking to one of the troopers: "Let's get that wound dressed."

They gave him water to drink and then Boag slipped away again. When he surfaced the sun was straight up in the sky and Captain McQuade came striding along the company street; the men were packing up their tents. Someone fed Boag and Captain McQuade crouched down on one knee. "How you making it, Boag?"

"I thought that was a dream, Captain. What you doing here?"

"According to you I'm still looking for Geronimo." Captain McQuade squinted at the sky. "We've got to keep moving, Boag, these hills are crawling with *federales*. Think you can sit a horse?"

"I guess I'll have to. The *rurales* are after me."

"What for?"

"I busted out of their jail down in Ures. Killed a couple of them."

"Boag you're incredible. Look, I'm heading south. Anywhere we can drop you?"

"Just so you don't drop me too hard, Captain, there's a ranch down south of here belongs to Don Pablo Ortiz."

"I think I know where that is."

"You going that way?"

"We can make a little detour."

"That's mighty kind of you, Captain."

"You're a hell of a soldier, Boag. If you pull out of this I'll want to talk to you again."

"Still trying to recruit me, hey?"

"I need a *segundo* with his head screwed on straight. My God, Boag, you don't know how bad I need that. Who put that slug in you? *Rurales?*"

"Prison guard, I reckon."

"Must have been a .45–90. Big sonofabitching hole in you, Boag."

"Well it's the second time this year I've been shot up on Mr. Pickett's account."

"Third time they won't shoot you up, boy, they'll shoot you down."

"There won't be no third time until I've got Mr. Pickett under a gun, Captain. I promise you that."

"You just get some rest, Boag. We'll rig a litter for you."

2

He didn't remember much of that trip either. They rigged a *travois* behind one of the horses and that was all right dragging on the pine needles but when they got down into dry country the damn thing started bouncing on rocks in the ground and it was holy hell. Boag passed out and didn't come to until nightfall.

Coffee with molasses in it. Some kind of thin soup. Toasted corn fritter. He got most of it down before he went under again.

Captain McQuade had some kind of Mexican medicine man who claimed to have been a medical orderly under Juarez. A wizened up old man with a deerskin pouch on a lanyard suspended from his neck. Herb potions and for all Boag knew crow-entrails. But when the son of a bitch cauterized Boag's wound with a fire-hot running-iron Boag was ready to kill him except the pain knocked him out before he could figure out how.

Next day at noon camp they pried his jaw open to feed him some solid meat in little tiny chunks. Captain McQuade said, "Almost there, Boag. Sometime tonight."

"Don't you boys ever sleep?"

"We've got a train to meet down on the Yaqui."

"You're always going to meet trains, Captain, ever' time I see you."

"Boag, there's nothing quite so satisfying in this life as the sight of a federal armored train blowing sky high off the tracks. It makes a marvelous potion for a jaded man. You want to try it sometime."

"Well that do sound like plenty of fun."

"Yes indeed it is. Those scabbed-up holes down in the calf of your leg, that the other time Pickett shot you?"

"That's right, Captain. They ain't very good shots as you can see."

"They hit you, didn't they?"

"They didn't kill me, and that was their mistake."

"Boag, you keep giving them enough practice and they'll get good enough to kill you."

"How come you keep trying to talk me out of this?"

"Because I think you're a damn fool to keep after Jed Pickett. You're biting off more than ten men can chew. I don't want you dead, Boag, I want you in my army."

"Must be plenty of mustered-out Buffalo soldiers you could hire, Captain."

"I'm sure there are. But you were the best combat soldier in the Tenth Cavalry. That's not flattery, that's God's truth. I even heard General Crook himself remark on one occasion that we could either send a squad of soldiers out to do a certain job or we could send Sergeant Boag."

"I never heard that before."

"Nobody wanted to give you a swelled head. When a man's a superb fighter you don't need to tell him about it, he knows it for himself."

"Yes sir, I know what I'm good at."

"You're good at soldiering. Right now I'm the only army you've got, Boag."

"You ain't the only war I've got."

"Why you're just doing this for the sheer hell of it, aren't you?"

"Captain, Mr. Pickett murdered my friend John B. Wilstach. I expect he owes me something on that account, not to mention some gold bullion we got in dispute."

"I recall Wilstach. Spent more time in the guardhouse than out."

"Well he was my friend, Captain."

"Making an ass out of yourself won't bring him back, will it?"

"I believe maybe it'll make him feel a little bit better, wherever he is."

"That's a pretty wild assumption to die for."

"You're sure as hell a stubborn man, Captain."

"Not half as stubborn as you." Captain McQuade got up on his feet. "Time to move out."

"Do me one more favor, Captain? Put me up on a saddle? That travvy's fixin' to shake me to pieces."

"I'll talk to the medico. If he says it's all right."

The wizened old medicine man came. Boag showed his distrust. The old man grinned through a few bad teeth that remained in the caved-in remains of his mouth; cackled and went away, and Boag felt very depressed but when they came to pick him up they put him on a blanket-draped saddle and Boag looked more kindly on the medicine man.

After the column started moving he changed his mind. If the *travois* had been pain, this was agony.

3

He was in and out of delirium for days. Afterward he decided it had something to do with safety, the disappearance of challenge. There was no immediate threat to him and so it was safe to go loose, to let the body take over; and simple impatience wasn't enough to overcome that. Every fiber went slack and he despised himself; he had never tolerated weakness in himself.

He dreamed frequently of the *señora;* he imagined her – naked, pink-brown, tender; his hands remembered the feel of her hard tight little ass and her velvet breasts.

"Stop that," she said. "Not now." She pushed his hand away.

He blinked up at her. He felt hung-over as hell. "Did I have a good time last night?"

"What?"

He recognized the room and recollection trickled into him. "Uh. How's Don Pablo?"

"He is the same."

"How am I?"

"You ought to be dead but you are not."

He didn't want to twist his head to look down at himself. "Is it mending?"

"Yes." She smiled slowly; her cross act had been fraudulent. "You have a very tough body."

"It's that black hide. Tough as armor."

He yelped when she pinched him. "Tough as armor," she said.

Then he slept again, warmed by the echo of her laughter. She must have bathed him because the prison stench was no longer in his nostrils. He had a picture of that scene and he wished he had been awake at the time.

Sometimes when he opened his eyes she was there; sometimes she wasn't. Sometimes there was daylight at the window. He had no way of counting the nights and days. He hovered in a kind of daydream for a very long time, not unconscious and yet not awake. Fevers sweated him and at times he was frozen through to the bones.

Once she said to him, "I am so glad you asked your friends to bring you back here."

"There was no other place to go. I'm sorry to be a burden. Now you have to look after two sick men."

"When I was a whore I dreamed of being a nurse." Her hand rested on him with a natural intimacy.

On another day Don Pablo came into the room and smiled when he saw Boag was awake. "You feel better now?"

"Getting better all the time," he said and instantly regretted it because it mocked Don Pablo's condition and he hadn't meant that; but an apology would only make it worse so he let it drift away uncorrected.

"Dorotea is very glad you chose our house for refuge."

"She said that."

"In a strange way I am glad too."

"Why?"

"We have very few friends any more. You chose this house because you thought of us as friends. It was the *señora* of course, it was not me; but nevertheless I am gratified. Can you understand this?"

"I think I can," Boag said and it occurred to him that with the possible exception of Captain McQuade—who had an axe to grind—he also had no other friends.

Then he thought of Pilar-Carmen, the little Yaqui girl. Was she his friend also? Perhaps she was. *I should look her up sometime.*

He said, "I owe you a debt now."

"Not at all. You have done us a kindness, as I have just explained."

"What if the troops come here looking for me? They find me here and you'll both be arrested."

"They will not look here. Why should it occur to them?"

"Suppose they arrest one of Captain McQuade's people and make him talk?"

"I think they seldom arrest the rebels any more. They do not take prisoners, Pesquiera's troops. They have an arrogance, they think they do not need to question prisoners any more; they expect to terrorize the province into obedience."

"Maybe."

"At any rate you shall stay as long as you need to. Do not feel any urgency about that."

"How long have I been here anyway?"

"Ten or eleven days, I forget exactly. I myself tend to disregard dates." Dorotea's husband touched Boag's arm and then walked to the door; paused there, and said before he left the room, "She is in love with you. I am sure you know that. I hope you will not grieve her. She should not have to lose both of her men at the same time."

"You sound like Captain McQuade," Boag growled, but the door was shut and he heard Don Pablo retreat through the courtyard, his retching cough sounding as though it were ripping the lining of his lungs away.

4

"I suppose the days give you time to think," Dorotea said. She lay against his good side and her cool hand slid up his chest.

"Well I get out of here, I expect I'll have to work out some way to find Mr. Pickett."

"Have you thought about why you do this?"

"I just have to, that's all."

"No, I do not think you have to. It is not pride and I do not really think it is revenge either."

Boag hitched himself up on one elbow and winced. "Everybody keeps telling me what I'm after. Don't you think I know? Your husband told me I was scared and he said I hated being scared so much I had to keep going out and proving it wasn't true."

"And?"

"He was wrong. I get scared—who doesn't?"

"But you invite it don't you? I mean who would care if you simply forgot about this gold and this man Pickett?"

"I'd care."

"Why? Does it really matter about the gold bullion or your friend who died?"

"Or Mr. Pickett's friends that put this bullet through me? Well maybe it don't. Captain McQuade keeps telling me I want an army to fight with."

"You are a fighting man. That is what you are."

"All right. But the war Captain McQuade's offering me, that ain't my war."

"And the war with this Pickett, that is your war?"

"Like I told Captain McQuade. It's the only war I've got." He reached for her hand and closed the big fist over it. "You been a kind of a slave, you know you just don't let them shove you around any more. That's what it is."

"Then your freedom is being in motion and keeping ahead of the bullets, is that what you mean?" She lay back against his arm; he thought she was smiling. "You are my adventurer," she said. "Big black soldier-of-fortune Boag."

5

By the second week of June it was full summer-hot and the grass was going yellow on the high plains. Boag was out of bed moving around as much as he could to rebuild the strength that had drained out of him as if a plug had been pulled. His right hip moved with a stiff awkwardness as if the ball didn't fit right into its socket any more: the .45-90 had taken some chips out of the hipbone. It didn't make him limp; it was more of a lurch.

Dorotea was amused. "You are the wreckage of a man. Now you have been shot in both legs."

"I'm lame but I'm still on my feet."

"And so brave," she breathed with wide-eyed mockery.

"Aagh."

He took one more turn around the courtyard and stopped at the front gate. Miguel stood there, ever vigilant, watching the valley through the view-port in the door. The old man's eyes were squinted in close-focused attention and Boag said, "Somebody coming."

"See for yourself, *Señor.*"

Miguel stepped aside lugging his shotgun and Boag looked through the hole.

It was a crowd of riders in a hurry.

"Coming straight for us."

"They ride like *soldados,*" Miguel said and Boag saw the sweat on his wrinkled face.

Boag felt himself tense up. The riders were still better than a mile out but they were drumming forward like a big locomotive at full throttle. A banner of dust raveled high in their wake.

"Where's my two pistols, Miguel?"

"Under the bed where you sleep."

Then Boag's shoulders dropped an inch. "It's all right. That's Captain McQuade."

"You have very good eyes, *Señor.*"

Dorotea crossed the court and Boag saw Don Pablo appear at his door on the veranda. Boag stepped through the gate and stood just outside it and waited for the horsemen.

They swirled to a halt. Hoofs churned up clots that spattered the adobe wall. Captain McQuade's grin cracked the coating of dust on his face. "So you made it. I expected you would."

"I'm still takin' nourishment," Boag acknowledged. "Light and set a while."

"Can't, Sergeant, we're in a little bit of a hurry."

"You got *federales* on your ass?"

"I think we shook them off. But there's a good big fight shaping up north of here. I'd hate to miss out on it."

Boag grinned.

"You well enough to ride?"

"It still ain't my fight, Captain."

"That's too bad. I'll talk you into it one of these days." Captain McQuade swept off his hat and dragged the crook of his elbow across his forehead. "There's two of Pickett's rawhiders hanging around the town of Tres Osos," he said, and replaced the hat square across his eyebrows.

"Thank you kindly, Captain."

"Well take it easy, Boag." And then they were moving: a rise and fall of Captain McQuade's arm, a looping wheel of two dozen horses, a thunder of hoof-fall.

Boag stepped inside and shut the door against the dust. Looking through the view-port he had a glimpse of the drag riders in Captain McQuade's troop: they were hauling a gun-cart and there was a ten-barrel Gatling gun mounted on it. Captain McQuade must have won a battle and taken that as part of the spoils.

In the twilight Don Pablo struggled down the stairs to the dining room where Miguel had set the table with their few plates and glasses arranged in formal patterns on the bare wood. Dorotea served up a meal that tasted very good to Boag.

Don Pablo was looking a little stronger than he had; it was possibly because there was color in his cheeks but that might have been the flush of fever, it was hard to tell.

Boag said, "How long before they throw you out of here?"

"Perhaps the end of this month. Perhaps my creditors will be kind and extend us a few weeks before we are dispossessed."

"Then I might as well get moving."

Dorotea rolled her eyes toward him. Don Pablo said, "You are not strong enough yet."

"I'm strong enough to ride. The rest will take care of itself in the saddle."

"But are you fast enough?"

"I never was fast. Just steady."

"You will need a little money I think. I have a little for you."

"You need to feed yourselves."

"There is enough for both."

"Then I won't dispute it. I'm obliged."

"It is we who are obliged," Don Pablo said.

But in the morning when Don Pablo came down one step at a time to watch Boag saddle the horse he said, "You will recall what was said the last time you rode away from here." He bent over to cough. "It still pertains."

"Other words, if I don't get some gold in my pockets you don't want me to come back."

"Not for Dorotea."

"Well you're her husband."

"I used to be," Don Pablo said. "Now I am her friend. I would not wish her to follow a dirt-poor Negro from town to town."

"What about a dirt-poor Castilian?"

Don Pablo considered it. In the end he conceded, "You have a point."

Boag smiled and went to say his *hasta luego* to the *señora.*

6

He didn't push himself; he used up four slow-riding days getting to Tres Osos. It was one of those *mestizo* towns high in the Sierra where most of the people had no Spanish, they talked an *Indio* dialect that Boag didn't understand.

The village welcomed him spectacularly: it was a Saturday afternoon and there was a wedding. The fiesta was accompanied by an earsplitting spectacle of Mexican fireworks and the entire population was turned out in elaborate costumes the women had probably spent a year making. It was a profusion of movement and color and noise. Boag sat on a rock up in the trees above the village, holding the reins of his horse, watching. He tried to disregard all the wheeling color; he was looking for two gringos not partaking of the festival.

He didn't see them for two hours. The village was a loose assemblage of huts that crawled down the corkscrew sides of a narrow canyon shaded by ranks of enormous pines that marched down the mountain like lancers with their weapons at the ready. The road ran close along the bank of the dry creek, wandering from one side of the canyon to the other. In seasons of heavy rain or during the spring thaw he expected not only the stream but the road also ran a foot deep in rushing water. Right now it was two months since the thaw and he didn't know of much rain since then, and the whole forest looked ready to go up in flame but the villagers were happily flinging their fireworks in the air with frivolous abandon and Boag watched with alarm as some of the sparks arced into the woods.

Late in the afternoon the honeymoon couple went away in a weathered buckboard and the fat women went back to their huts and the men settled down in the plaza for some industrious drinking.

The air stank of sulphur smoke as if a battle had been fought. The church bells had quit ringing and the yelling was done; everyone had gone hoarse. The silence seemed unnatural. In that atmosphere Boag saw the two rawhiders emerge from the shade of a pine copse beside a corral that contained four or five horses and several burros. They must have been there all the time, sitting with their backs to the corral fence watching the show.

They walked across the plaza into a square hut. Boag watched the place patiently. Within three minutes the rawhiders reappeared in the doorway. One of them had a small jug so that hut must be the *cantina.*

Some old men on the plaza shouted at the rawhiders, inviting them to take part in the remnants of the feast. The two rawhiders went over to them and sat down on the ground to eat. There was a thin one and a fat one. Boag remembered the fat one; he believed the fat one went by the name of Jackson.

By the time the rawhiders finished eating it would be pretty dark. Jackson and his friend would probably finish their small jug on the plaza and then perhaps they would return to the *cantina* for another jug and a game of cards or monte or darts. They would do that because there was nothing else to do in a village like this and it was clear the two men were waiting for something that wasn't going to happen right away. Either they were hiding out or they were waiting for someone to arrive and meet them.

At any rate the thing to do was to get inside the *cantina* and wait for them there.

Boag led his horse back into the trees and began to make a wide circle through the forest to come up behind the *cantina.* He hoped the place had a back door.

7

The weedy ground behind the *cantina* was strewn with broken jugs and bits of splintered woodwork, the souvenirs of lusty brawls. It smelled of urine.

There was a back door and Boag opened it without announcing himself.

There was no real bar. A big plank table served. Jugs were cluttered on it and a half-asleep proprietor sat in a chair behind the table. He had a little wooden box with coins in it. Probably he had a brewing shack and a small distillery back in the woods near a spring.

Two Indians at a table watched Boag enter the room. Nobody seemed surprised, let alone alarmed. It was the kind of place where it took a great deal to arouse people.

Boag bought a small jug and settled down behind a table facing the front door.

Someone outside had brought a guitar and the rapid-fire music reached Boag faintly. There were occasional bursts of laughter in the night; now and then a footstep moved by, and Boag would stiffen and fasten his eyes on the door. Three townsfolk came in and settled at a front table to play cards. The two Indians finished their jug and left the place. The proprietor's face was tilted in disgust as he contemplated the contents of his wooden box. Here it was Saturday night but most everybody was played-out by the wedding festival and the *cantina's* trade was shot to hell.

Boag heard boots with spurs on them and he knew it was Jackson and his *compadre.* He made his simple preparations and watched them walk in.

They didn't see him at first. They were off guard, Jackson was telling a story:

". . . and she says to Ben Stryker, she says 'That man wanted to give me four dollars to sleep with him!' and old Ben pulls his iron on the boy and puts two good ones right in his balls. And you know what Ben Stryker did then? He says, 'I reckon that'll be a lesson for rich boys that try to come down here and double the price of everthang.' "

They were both bent over laughing their guts out when Jackson picked up Boag in the corner of his vision. Jackson went bolt still and straightened up very slowly. It took his partner a little longer to catch on and then the partner gave Jackson a puzzled look.

Jackson said, "Now, I know you."

"I'm Boag."

"That's mighty nice of you. I expect you've got a gun under that table."

"Two of them."

"You think that's fair, boy?"

"I count two of you."

Sweating, Jackson wiped his palms dry on his buttocks. He was a sag-bellied suety man with droopy jowls and big hard hands. His face was covered with dust and insect bites.

Boag said, "You gents might shuck your irons and sit down here."

Jackson hesitated and his partner looked at him, but it was all right; Jackson had made up his mind when he hadn't started for his gun the moment he'd recognized Boag.

Jackson unbuckled his belt carefully and hung it over the back of the nearest chair, waited for his partner to do the same and then they both walked up to Boag's table, dragged chairs over with their toes and sat down slowly as if they were afraid the chairs were about to explode under their butts.

Boag said, "I know Jackson. What do you go by?"

"Smith."

"Sure enough," Boag said. "You folks want a drink?" He nodded his head toward the jug in the middle of the table and Jackson nodded his head and reached out for the jug. Jackson took a swallow and set the jug down. He didn't offer it to Smith. He just sat turning the jug casually in his fingers, thinking about throwing it in Boag's face, and Boag said, "Let that thing alone unless you're ready to drink from it."

"I'd sure like to try you on, boy."

"You won't get the chance," Boag said. "One white trash more or less ain't worth dying for. I ain't got time to waste in disputations with you."

He was watching Smith out of the edge of his eye. A corded muscle tensed under Smith's shirt sleeve; his hand was easing toward the edge of the table. Boag reached across and grabbed Smith's shirt-front and pulled Smith's face down onto the tabletop. Smith's teeth clicked, his jaw sagged, his eyes rolled up.

Jackson said drily, "You lied about one of them guns."

"No, I left it in my lap."

"Maybe you lied about both of them."

"You got one quick way to find out, fat man." Boag smiled amiably. "I got one in here with your name on it, Jackson."

"What you got against me, boy? What I ever do to you?"

"Sure. Now you can tell me you weren't one of those guns shooting at me from the riverboat when I went in the water."

"What if I was? You asked for that."

"'Course I did," Boag muttered. "Now let's talk about Mr. Pickett a while."

Smith was sitting up. Groggy. Fingering his jaw. His Adam's apple rode up and down his throat in spasms; his thin face looked sick. "Christ I think you bust my jaw."

"No," Boag said. "But it'll hurt to chew for a week or so. You better stick to soft food."

He went back to the fat one: "I said let's talk about Mr. Pickett."

"What about him?"

"I ain't greedy, Jackson, I don't want more than you got. All I want is the name of a place."

"What place?"

"Where I can find Mr. Pickett."

Smith snickered and winced and touched his jaw very gently.

Jackson said, "Listen, he double-crossed us the same way he double-crossed you. He tooken off with the gold, him and Ben Stryker and Gutierrez and a couple others. The rest of us scattered and hid out on account we didn't want them gunning after us one by one."

Boag smiled a little. "And you expect me to buy that right off the shelf."

"It's the truth, I can't hep it. Smith, you tell him."

"I ain't likely to believe him more than you," Boag said. "Now why don't we try it again. Pretend like I asked the same question and you get to answer it like you never heard it before."

"Boy, the trouble with you, you don't wear your hat square on your head. You think we'd be up here in this miserable hole if we had some of that gold to spend?"

"Why don't you just tell me why you're up here in this miserable hole."

"I told you boy, we hiding out from Pickett's guns."

Boag sighed. "How long you been riding for Mr. Pickett, Jackson? Twenty years?"

"Twenty-three. And the thanks I get— —"

"Let's us go up in the woods a ways," Boag said. "We'll set and jaw." He rammed one of the revolvers into his belt and plucked the jug off the table. "We'll take this here for company."

He stood up waggling the revolver in his right hand. "Back door, gents."

They went out the door ahead of him and they were ready to jump him when he came through it but he jabbed the pistol-barrel hard into Jackson's diaphragm and Jackson folded up on the ground and sucked for breath. Boag wheeled toward Smith but Smith wasn't fighting, he was slithering back inside.

Boag whipped around the doorframe but Smith had reached the table just inside. Smith batted the table back at him and it hit Boag between the knees and the crotch. It didn't knock him down but it pushed him back from the door and by the time he got in the doorway again and shoved the table aside Smith was diving at the chair where his gunbelt hung. He knocked the chair over with him and went sliding along the floor trying to fumble the six-gun out of leather. Boag was wary of Jackson behind him but he tried to sight a clear shot through the tables and chairs. He didn't get one before Smith got hold of the gun; Smith was shooting through the toe of the holster and that was no aid to accuracy and after Smith's second bullet punched into the doorjamb Boag got an unobstructed line on his neck and put a bullet into it.

He didn't wait to see its effect; what he aimed at, he hit. He spun backward through the door and cocked the revolver and let his voice sing out loud toward the wide round backside of Jackson who was scrambling up toward the pines. "*Freeze.*"

Jackson stopped and turned. He looked unhappy as a soaked cat.

"Come on back here."

Jackson started to waddle and Boag flattened his shoulderblades against the wall beside the open door in case Smith still had enough blood in him to come after him.

Boag said, "Run, you fat trash. Run."

Jackson started to lope. His belly flopped up and down and his arms pumped. He was short of breath by the time he came up; it had only been thirty yards. Boag said, "Go on inside ahead of me." He pushed his gun into Jackson's kidney and marched him inside with an armlock around Jackson's fat throat.

The shield was unnecessary. Smith wasn't dead yet but he

hadn't moved six inches from where he'd fallen. The three card-players and the proprietor hadn't stirred; they watched Boag with no show of friendliness but no show of threat either. These were all outsiders to them and they didn't care who killed whom, so long as no citizens got stray lead.

Boag hauled Jackson outside again. "You got a horse in that corral up there?"

"I reckon."

"Let's go saddle up then."

"Wait a minute. Can't we talk here?"

"I don't think we want to be disturbed."

"I'd just as soon not leave this town."

"Well you ain't got a vote, Jackson. Now let's go get your horse."

Boag picked a spot back in the mountains six or seven miles away from Tres Osos. He hobbled his horse and hobbled Jackson's horse and then he unlashed Jackson's wrists from the saddlehorn and let Jackson step down. While Jackson rubbed some circulation back into his hands Boag loosened the cinches and carried Jackson's rifle over to a flat slab of rock. "Come on over here. Bring my canteen."

"Canteen?"

"Just bring it, stupid."

It was a clear night, part of a moon and plenty of stars. It took Jackson's clumsy hands a long time to untie the canteen. He brought it with him. Boag pointed to a little bowl-shaped depression in the slab of granite. "Empty it in there."

"All of it?"

"There's plenty of springs up here. Nobody'll go thirsty."

Jackson emptied it into the bowl. The water gurgled ominously. It made a little pool of motionless liquid a foot in diameter and four or five inches deep.

Boag cut a six-foot length of rope and tossed it to him. "Tie your ankles together now. I'm going to check it afterward so you may as well make it good and tight the first time."

"What the hell you up to, boy?"

"Quit calling me boy, Jackson. Just because you outweigh me by forty pounds of lard."

"What you got in mind here?"

"Never you mind. You just do what you're told."

"Why?"

"Because I got this gun pointed at your ass, you stupid trash."

Jackson sat down with a grunt and doubled his knees up under his chin and wrapped the rope around his ankles. Boag watched him cinch it up and tie a double bowline knot in it. Boag said, "You're pretty good with knots."

"I've hung a few nigger boys in my time."

"You ain't making friends with me that way."

"You can go fuck yourself, boy."

"Lay down on your belly," Boag said. He took the rope he'd used on Jackson's wrists before; he tied Jackson's arms together, sitting on Jackson's buttocks while he yanked the tie up tight. Jackson's cheek was pressed into the rough surface of the rock; Jackson said, "Hey."

"Well I'm sorry we ain't got no feather pillows." When Boag was satisfied with the tie he climbed off the man. "You can roll over and set up."

Jackson showed his distress but he managed to heave himself onto his back and sit up without scraping too much skin off his hands. He glanced at the little pool of water a few yards off to his left.

"Now you're hogtied and sweatin' and you don't know for sure what's coming next. I'd tell you but it might spoil the fun. I'll just tell you this much. You can save yourself whatever it is by telling me where I can find Mr. Pickett."

"I told you, boy. You just don't listen. I got no idea where he's at."

Boag decided to save the pool of water a while. Lead up to it first. He walked over to Jackson and hunkered down and put his palms flat against Jackson's jowly cheeks. Held his thumbs over Jackson's eyes and pressed slowly. Enough of it and it would crush in Jackson's eyeballs. He kept increasing the pressure until Jackson screamed.

He relaxed his thumbs. "Aeah?"

"Cut that out, you son of a bitch."

"What about Mr. Pickett then?"

"I can't tell you nothing I don't know!"

Boag put the pressure on again.

9

Jackson's chest heaved for breath. "All right boy. All right."

"All right who?"

"Just all right."

"I'll tell you what, Jackson, you call me Sergeant Boag, all right?"

"If you say so."

"If you say so who?"

"If you say so, Sergeant Boag."

"Now let Sergeant Boag hear where Mr. Pickett's camped."

"Last I heard he was up one of them little towns above Ures on the Sonora River, waitin' to meet up with some fellow from Mexico City was going to take the gold off his hands for New York bank scrip."

"Selling the same gold all over again, is he?"

"How's that?"

"He already sold it once to a fellow name of Ortiz."

"Yeah. How'd you know about that? Jesus my eyes hurt. I think I'm blind."

"You'll have a hell of a headache for a couple days," Boag said. "You'll think somebody jammed a wad of barbwire inside your skull."

"Boy you want carvin' up. I get a chance I'm gon bust a big hole in you, Sergeant Boag sir."

There was still too much defiance in Jackson and that was what convinced Boag he was still lying. There was no point questioning him any further until he'd been softened up some more. Jackson was big and soft but he had a great capacity for pain and Boag wasn't getting the truth out of him.

Boag took him by the arm. "Come over here with me." He brought Jackson along on his knees and positioned him belly-flat on the rock. Jackson had to hold his chin up to keep his face out of the pool of water. Every time he tried to wriggle to one side Boag pushed him back into position.

"What you think now, Jackson?"

"For God's sake I already told you what you want to know."

"Maybe you'll change your mind after a while of this."

With red-hot hate Jackson reared his head back. "By God boy— —"

Boag shoved his face down into the water and felt it when Jackson's nose hit the bottom of the pool. He held the back of Jackson's head and sat on Jackson's spine to keep him from rolling away. Jackson's legs came up from the knee hinges but Jackson couldn't reach Boag with his spurs. Boag held his head under until bubbles started coming up. Then he hauled Jackson's head back by the hair.

Jackson blew and snorted and heaved for breath. Boag said, "God damn it you got chiggers in your hair. Don't you ever take a bath, white trash?" He let go of Jackson's head and batted at his hand.

Then when Jackson exhaled he shoved Jackson's face in the water again.

He let Jackson get panicky this time before he let go. Jackson's head skewed back and he spouted a spray of water. He coughed a lot and started to retch into the water and when he was all through being sick, Boag shoved his face in it again.

This time he let Jackson get his breath afterward.

"Let's try a different question this time, fat boy. Why'd Mr. Pickett send you two gents up to Tres Osos?"

"Look after," Jackson said and coughed, "the gold."

"You mean you got the gold up here in Tres Osos with you?"

"Some of it. It's scattered, some of the boys got some of the gold. A lot of different towns—a dozen maybe." Jackson wheezed and coughed.

"So all the gold ain't in one place for somebody to steal it away. Mr. Pickett's sure a cautious man."

Agony pulled at Jackson's mouth; he gulped like a fresh-caught fish. "He's got a big safe coming up from Mexico City. They building him a vault. They get it built, the gold comes in, that's the idea."

"Where's this vault at?"

"I don't rightly remember."

Boag pushed on the back of his head and immersed his face and held it there until he saw the muscles of the neck begin to bulge. He let Jackson sputter and gag and shoved him under water again. He did it five times in all before he spoke again:

"Try me on that vault of Mr. Pickett's now."

All these efforts were painful for Boag. The .45-90 wound in his hip was bad and even the old hole through his calf was troublesome. He'd pushed himself a little too hard. Now he was impatient with Jackson's bravery. Perhaps it communicated itself to Jackson; the fiight trickled out of the fat man. He talked in a weary fast drone.

"You know where Santa Cruz Creek starts?"

"No."

"Up in the mountains a ways south of Coronado."

"You mean way back in the Sierra Madre."

When Jackson spoke he wheezed and sputtered a lot. "Yeah. All right, a few mile northwest of the lakes. There's a real old silver mine up there. Must be two hundred years old.

They had a lot of Innun trouble in those days, they built those mines like Cavalry forts. Some kind of high old rock wall around the thing. Sets up there on a flat-top mountain and they ain't but one way in or out of there, it's a kind of steep cut in the cliff with a wagon road goes down it."

"And that's where Mr. Pickett's at?"

"I got no idea if that's where he's at now. It's where we was supposed to bring the gold to. Where the vault is. Christ, you mind if I slide over a bit? I'm getting mighty tired holding my chin up like this."

"We'll just wait on you to get all finished talking first."

"Jesus Boag, I told you what you wanted."

Boag pushed his face in the water.

The idea was to keep up the pressure until you kept getting the same answer every time. With a liar like Jackson you had to make sure.

Laced with his own hurts Boag kept it up for another half hour until he was satisfied Jackson was telling something that approximated the truth.

After a while Jackson became eager to talk because as long as he was talking his face wasn't in the pool. But Boag caught him lying twice and shoved him back in mid-sentence, and soon Jackson was talking with care. But talking.

"Pickett's fixing to set himself up like a tinpot Napoleon over there in that district," Jackson explained, and wheezed and spat to catch his breath. "Using that gold to start buying up all kinds of properties. This revolution going on, a lot of them old *dons* scared shitless. They eager to get hard money for their *ranchos.* All they want to do is beat it out of Mexico. Time he's through, Jed Pickett's gon own half of the state of Sonora."

"Well six feet of it anyway."

Jackson said, "You got a large opinion of yourself, boy."

"Who?"

"Sergeant Boag. Whatever you want to be called. Your skin won't be worth tanning, time Jed Pickett gets through with you. I'd admire to see that, too."

"You and Smith was supposed to take your piece of the

gold on down to Mr. Pickett's place in the Santa Cruz district, that right?"

"I just got done telling you that."

"When was this supposed to be?"

"We supposed to show up there this comin' Friday. We was fixing to leave maybe Tuesday afternoon, Wednesday morning."

"All right. Now where's your cache, Jackson?"

"Never you mind."

Boag's nostrils dilated. "Time you went back in that pool, get your face washed again."

"Sergeant Boag sir, I ain't going to tell you where that gold's at. You wouldn't have no more use for me alive."

"This gon be a mighty painful Saturday night for you then, fat trash."

"I expect it will."

"Then I may as well kill you right now if there ain't nothing else you want to tell me."

"Oh I don't think you'll do that, Sergeant Boag, sir."

"Well," Boag said, and slammed Jackson's face down into the water.

All the splashing had half-emptied the little pool but there was still enough to cover Jackson's nose and mouth. Boag kept grinding his face against the rock. It took a while but finally Jackson gave in.

"All right, all right. I'll show you where it's at."

"Like hell you will. You'll tell me."

"It's hard to explain."

"You just try."

He had Jackson explain it three or four times until he was pretty sure he had the idea. Then he roped Jackson to a tree and went looking for the gold.

The moon slid one way and clouds moved the other way across it. *You go out back of town and there's some old greaser's shack up in them trees with a bunch of roses in the yard.* Bats dived from tree to tree; a flock of chickens ran across Boag's path. *Back of the house there's some aspen. You go around them, you find a half acre of bald-headed boulders.* A bobcat leaped away, flushed by

Boag's approach. Boag dismounted. His boots scraped the limestone. The breeze was thin and cool. *You find a boulder higher than your head shaped kind of like a soldier's shako hat. Kind of flat on top but tilted over to one side.* Boag didn't have any trouble finding it by moonlight. It loomed against the forest beyond, a pale monument against the heavy mass of dark trees.

He had a stick he used as a cane to walk across the rocks. When he reached the shako boulder he started poking under it with the stick because he didn't want to be surprised by a sleepy rattler. He kept poking until he knew it would have disturbed any poison critter sleeping there. Then he got down on his knees and almost cried out from the pain and used his hands to paw the rocks and pebbles out of the hole.

It took a while. Finally he got down to the canvas sacks. He poked some more with the stick and a scorpion went scuttling away, making a little scratching racket on the rocks. He let it get a good piece away from him before he did any more prospecting.

"Now don't that beat all."

He hadn't really believed Jackson but here it was. Two gunny sacks, maybe seventy-five pounds of weight in each one of them. Boag did figures in his head. "Maybe thirty-thousand dollars American. Well Hallelujah."

He lugged it back over to the horse one sack at a time because he was nowhere near being in shape to carry both at once.

It made a heavy load for the horse. He'd have to ride slow and easy.

He headed up into the mountains. There was no point going back to where he'd left Jackson tied up. The fat trash would work himself loose sooner or later. Or he wouldn't.

It had occurred to him maybe he ought to put Jackson on his horse and tell him to ride up into Santa Cruz and tell Mr. Pickett what had happened up here tonight. It would be good in a number of ways to have Mr. Pickett know. Tell Jackson to give Mr. Pickett a message: "Tell him he'll be seeing me all of a sudden." Over a gunsight.

It had appeal. Get Mr. Pickett angry as hell. When a man got angry he made mistakes. It would have been nice.

But Jackson wouldn't have done it. Jackson wasn't about to go back to Mr. Pickett now. He'd have to tell Mr. Pickett how Boag got the best of him and Smith and got away with Mr. Pickett's gold. Mr. Pickett wouldn't like that at all; he'd take Jackson apart in pieces and throw the pieces in Santa Cruz Creek. No, Jackson would stay as far away from the rawhiders as he could get. So there was no point turning him loose. Let him take his chances. He'd maybe get loose, and if he did he'd be like the other white trash, like Frailey back on the Colorado River who'd shrugged his losses and taken off for California to try his luck. These rawhiders didn't have much sand except when they were mobbed together in the big gang. Then they were tough enough.

Tough enough, he thought. He had a lot of gold on his saddle right now and the smart thing would be to take it and get shet of Sonora. That little business he'd been planning to start, up in Oregon or somewhere. He had plenty of money for that now. To hell with Mr. Pickett, to hell with the *Señora* Dorotea Ortiz. Boag had his share and he had about a thousand percent interest on it.

Why push your luck?

You went along most of the time like a damn fool letting impulse push you around. Once in a while a small voice inside you said, "Quit this foolishness."

Boag heard the small voice. He didn't obey it.

chapter seven

1

In the morning he came to a town where people were just emerging from the church, shorn of sin and renewed for another week. The women all had shawls over their heads and the men were putting their hats on. Boag doubted God had much interest in their prayers but he had no objection; they had to feel they could do something that would protect themselves.

He rode through the town with Jackson's .41 Remington rifle across his saddlebow. He was looking for a livery stable because he wanted to buy a pack horse to carry the gold; his own horse was game enough but this weight would wear it out soon.

The town had no livery but he was directed by the blacksmith to a ranch north of the village and because it was not out of his way he stopped there and bargained with a sweating old man who finally sold him an eight-year-old mare and a crosstree pack saddle.

He packed his way north along the ridgetops, riding the military crest to keep off the skyline. From here he could see west across the flats of the river valleys; he was looking and listening for signs of battle because he needed a certain amount of ordnance and matériel to make his fanciful schemes work, and a battlefield was the likely place to look.

Monday afternoon he observed a light skirmish along the Yaqui River but there was nothing going off except rifles. He didn't hang around.

Early Tuesday morning he judged he was close enough to the Santa Cruz country. He cached almost all the gold by making a little mud-and-rock dam across part of a thin stream, digging a hole, burying the gold, and then breaking the dam up so that the water flowed back across its original channel with the gold under it.

He marked the spot in his memory and knew he wouldn't have trouble finding it again; there was a twisted pine on the north side of the creek and a top-heavy boulder on the south bank and the gold was buried on the line of sight between them.

He kept one ingot with him. It was a partial ingot, the kind the smelters stamped out one at a time when they didn't have enough gold to complete a run on the main stamp press. It probably weighed twelve or fourteen pounds and it had to be worth at least twenty-five hundred dollars; it was a little bigger than Boag's fist.

He spent the day chasing around the high country seeking vantage points from which to view the wide Mexican plains. Still looking for a battle. He didn't find any. Maybe the revolution had quieted down but more likely it was just the law of averages; you couldn't be more than one place at one time and the odds weren't too good there'd be a battle there at that time.

By nightfall he was a little jittery because time was getting tight. He wanted to hit those messengers with their gold before they got it into Mr. Pickett's vault.

He had a piece of luck. Sundown—he was about to give up and pitch camp when he spotted movement down near the river. A thousand feet lower in elevation and a good many miles away. It was dust on the road, the kind that had to come from the hoofs of a pretty big column of riders. Anything smaller and Boag wouldn't have seen it at that distance.

He rode toward it. They might shoot at him just for target practice but then again they might have something Boag could use.

2

"You independent son of a bitch," Captain Shelby McQuade said by way of greeting.

"You want to tell these picket guards of yours to point them rifles at somebody else, Captain?"

Captain McQuade made hand gestures and the two sentries who'd prodded Boag into camp lowered their rolling-blocks and turned away to go back to their posts. "Eyes like eagles, these guard dogs of yours," Boag said, dismounting stiff in all his joints. "I practically had to announce my name before they knowed I was there."

"Lazy turds," Captain McQuade growled. "I have to kick ass every half hour."

"You got a pretty big army here now, though."

The Mexicans were setting up a few tents along the river-bank. Most of them didn't bother with tents or didn't have any; they were unrolling their saddle blankets on the hot dry ground. Boag's eye had had a good many years' practice estimating the size of a military unit with a single glance. He figured this one close to regiment size.

"We won a couple of fights up above Ures. A lot of recruits came in. We even got a few coming over from the Pesquiera army."

"Then at least you got some professional help."

Captain McQuade snorted. "Rotten excuses for soldiers. That's why we're whipping the pants off them."

"Are you now?"

"Well we would be if it wasn't for your friend Jed Pickett, I think." Captain McQuade lifted the flap of his command tent and ducked inside; Boag followed him. There was a cot and a folding desk with a lantern on it and Captain McQuade shook the lantern to check the fuel before he put a match to it and adjusted the wick. "We had a good one two days ago up there. We killed some, and then we set up an ambush because I knew they'd be back—these Papists never leave their dead, they always come back for them. So we killed some more."

"You could play that trick once too often."

"Sure, I know that Boag," Captain McQuade said. "How's Don Pablo and the missus?"

"All right."

"When'd you see them last?"

"About a week ago."

"Around here that can be a long time."

Boag slapped his hat against his thigh to beat the dust from it. "What's this you said about Mr. Pickett mixing into your war?"

"He's backing Pesquiera, I hear. Trying to shore up the regime."

"What for?"

"Pickett's buying up a lot of land for pennies on the peso. I think he's got empire plans, he wants to be the czar of the Santa Cruz district. But it's against Mexican law for any foreigner to own more than forty-nine percent of any income-producing property. They want to keep foreign capital from taking over the country. So your friend Pickett's putting the land in the name of one of his men, a Mexican."

"Gutierrez."

"That's it. Gutierrez is just a dummy front for Pickett and everybody knows it. The government could hit him for fraud and take it all away from him. If we win this revolution and Cesar Ruiz takes over the Governor's Palace down in Hermosillo your friend Pickett is out on his ass. So Pickett's paying a lot of money into the Governor's treasury and the Governor's using it to buy new batches of field pieces and Gatling guns. It makes the hill a lot harder for us to climb."

"Then you'd feel a lot better if you could get Mr. Pickett out of this thing. Right Captain?"

"Now you're the one that wants me to join your army, that it?" Captain McQuade laughed a little but his long face settled back into lines that seemed even more dour than usual. His eyes had an ominous murky color; he seemed unnaturally tired. He uncorked a jug and offered it to Boag: pure tequila, the kind that burned all the way down.

"I'm sorry Boag. For one thing Pickett's a civilian and that puts him out of my reach. But for another thing I've got a campaign going here and I haven't got time chasing off with you after some pipe dream of glory. I guess you're still in a real sweat to get killed, aren't you."

"Captain I ain't asking you to fight my war for me. But I need a little backing. Logistical. I think it'd be worth your while on the chance it would take him out. Mr. Pickett."

"What kind of logistical backing, Boag?"

"Mainly one of them Gatling guns you got."

"I'm sorry. That's out of the question."

"I'd be pleased to pay for it. I can lead you to twenty-five hundred dollars real quick-like. You get the money first, then I take the Gatling gun. Just a loan for a little spell, you understand. You'll get the gun back but you keep the twenty-five hundred dollars. You boys need money don't you? That's a pretty high rental fee."

He never trusted anyone entirely. He had the money right outside in his saddlebag, the half brick of gold, but he wasn't about to admit that.

"I'll have to think on that," Captain McQuade said. "We need every gun, Boag."

"Twenty-five hundred dollars U.S., Captain."

"I'll think on it. You had any grub tonight?"

"Not yet."

"Neither have I. Let's fit our bellies around something."

3

The coffee smoked as it poured into Boag's cup; it made a good smell. He was reminded of the musky smell of Dorotea's breasts.

"You've got twenty-five hundred dollars," Captain McQuade said. "Why don't you quit? Even a train stops."

"Well I still got a thing or two to settle with Mr. Pickett."

"It gravels me to see a good man ask for killing. You're just standing out there like Custer, Boag. Pickett's just waiting for you to get a little closer to him so he can stick it in your back and break it off."

"It wouldn't be the first time he tried that. I found those two rawhiders of his down to Tres Osos. I'm obliged to you for the word on that."

"That where you got all this money you're waving around at me?"

"Aeah."

"Well that bought you a little time, I guess."

"That's all any of us got, Captain. A little time between birth and death."

"Don't you go wise man on me, Boag. Look, join up with me. Between us we'll get rid of Pesquiera and that'll put the slide under Jed Pickett. We're both on the same side of this. And God knows I still need you. All I've got around here is fools with cranberries for *cojones*."

"It still ain't my war, Captain."

"Now quit waving your conscience around. You want Pickett a lot worse than I do."

"And I'm gon get him. But my way, Captain."

Captain McQuade rubbed the back of his head, bobbing and ducking his head. Very tired. Finally he said, "Well I'm sorry Boag but I can't let you have a ten-barrel gun. We're short of them and besides if yours fell into Pickett's hands that would be one more Gatling out against us. But you got anything else I can provide?"

"A few things I could use. A coil of heavy-gauge wire. A few kegs of blasting powder. Maybe half a dozen rifles. A few hundred rounds ammunition. A couple good hundred-foot lassos. One first-rate long-range rifle. Thirty-eight fifty-six if you got one. I had one but they took it off me in Ures. A few gallons of kerosene, a couple blankets. A buckboard to carry it all. And maybe you could cut me out a horse to haul the wagon."

"Boag you're putting me ass-deep in requisitions." Captain McQuade looked pained. "I've got damn little to spare in this camp."

"I'll pay you for it, Captain."

Captain McQuade did not stir; only the eyes moved. They settled on Boag with enormous disgust. Captain McQuade picked up a twig and burrowed it into his ear and examined it and threw it away, and in the end he said, "I can let you have the kerosene. The blankets and the lassos, all right. I can probably even scare up a few beat-up carbines and a little ammunition. If I can find any construction wire I'll let you have a roll. But a good long rifle and blasting powder and a buckboard? Those I can't spare, Boag."

It was what Boag had expected but he had tried it first; you had to.

He stood up and raised the tent flap to look outside. Then he turned back and when Captain McQuade lifted the ruby coals of his eyes, Boag flicked out a revolver and cocked it with a series of ominous clicks. "Let me see your holster gun a minute, Captain."

"What the hell?"

Boag took the revolver from him. Emptied it and handed it back to Captain McQuade.

"Aw Boag," Captain McQuade said in disgust.

"Well I'm sorry Captain. If I had another way I'd do it."

"You won't get ten feet from here. Not alive."

"Sure I will. Because nobody's going to know about it except you and me, and you ain't going to talk up."

"Why won't I?"

"Because I just unloaded your gun, Captain, and I got mine pointed at you, and if you hear a loud noise it will be you dying."

"They'll know, Boag. They'll shoot you full of holes."

"Not as long as I stick close to you like a burr. Captain they need you so bad they can taste it. You're a first-class soldier and they ain't got another one like you in all of Sonora. They can't afford to open up shooting if you could get hit. So it ain't much risk for either of us so long as you play by my rules. It ain't going to hurt you, all you'll lose is a little sleep."

"Boag if you knew how much sleep was worth to me right now. . . ."

"Sure enough. Well now you can pucker up your asshole and walk out of here right in front of me. I ain't gon show my gun but it'll be right handy if I need it. All you got to do is tell your boys to rustle up that order of mine. Including the Gatling gun."

Captain McQuade tipped his head just a little bit to one side. He watched Boag and didn't say anything. It was as if he was waiting to wake up from a tedious dream. Out on the picket line Boag could hear the light thud of hoof, the swish of tail.

"Come on now Boag, you're not going to shoot me."

"Captain I'll shoot your ears off one at a time and then I'll go for your kneecaps. You won't be able to ride, let alone walk. You try me."

"What the hell. I thought you were a friend of mine."

"Another time I'll apologize for this, Captain."

Captain McQuade went toward the tent flap. Boag said, "Kindly don't tell me I won't get away with it."

"You don't mind if I think it, do you?" Captain McQuade's face was composed into lines indicative of mild scorn but it seemed directed at himself as much as at Boag. He batted the tent flap back and Boag went outside with him.

4

The wind ruffled the blue lining of Captain McQuade's cape. Boag stood close behind him and watched the troops load the wagon, grunting under the weight of the powderkegs and the dismounted Gatling gun. Gnats and flies swarmed around a dribble of horse dung near Boag's feet.

A Mexican brought Boag's horse along and Boag told him to tie it to the tailboard of the wagon.

Boag said, "You drive, Captain."

"That's what I thought."

"Look, I'll turn you loose, it'll be a couple hours' walk back here. Ain't no big thing."

"Damn it Boag, I need some sleep. If I don't get some sleep I swear I'm going to perish."

"We get out of camp here, I'll drive the wagon. You can sleep. That sound all right?"

Captain McQuade hauled himself up onto the high seat and Boag settled beside him. "I hope they don't try to follow me," Boag said. "They ain't good enough."

Captain McQuade said to a lieutenant, "I'm doing a reconnoitre with the scout here. I'll be back sometime tonight. Keep this camp secure and tell them not to shoot my ass off when I get back, all right?"

Captain McQuade lifted the reins and made noises at the horse and Boag put one hand on the edge of the seat to keep from being pitched off. The wagon bucked out of camp and Boag said, "Upstream a ways and then we'll turn east up the mountains."

When the fires of the camp fell away behind them Boag took the reins and Captain McQuade leaned forward with his elbows braced on his splayed knees. His head hung down and swayed. By God he really was asleep.

Boag did his best to avoid the big bumps. He rode the buckboard up into the mountains and somewhere around midnight he stopped the wagon and climbed down, went back to his horse behind the tailboard and got the hunk of gold out of the saddlebag. Then he shook Captain McQuade by the shoulder. "This where you get off."

Captain McQuade gave him a drunken look. "Uh?"

"Come on, Captain."

"Where the hell are we?"

"You just head west and keep going downhill, you'll hit the river down there. Turn left, go downstream you'll walk right into your camp. Take you two-three hours from here."

Captain McQuade climbed down; Boag gave him a hand. "Here, stick this in your pocket."

"What's—?"

"I said I'd pay you for the stuff."

"Jesus."

"I'll get the Gatling gun back to you if I can."

"This honest-to-God gold?"

"Yes sir. You don't want to spend it all in one saloon."

"Right now I could just about do that."

"Captain you better wake up. You don't want some bandit taking that hunk of gold away from you. And don't forget to load up that gun I emptied." Boag climbed onto the seat and settled the reins among his fingers. "Good luck in your war, Captain."

Captain McQuade just glared at him and Boag drove the wagon on up the slope.

But after a little while when he looked back he saw Captain McQuade raising an arm to wave. "Good luck in yours too, Boag."

5

Morning was a bad time. You woke innocent and then you remembered last night. That had been a bad trick to play on a friend.

And remembering last night you superimposed it on

today: you remembered how you had invited getting all shot to pieces by a regiment and you knew the good fortune of the escape might not be granted you again today.

Boag checked out the load on the wagon and tied his saddle horse to the tailboard again and headed the buckboard for the Santa Cruz district.

Last night he had spent a couple of hours wiping out his sign so that if Captain McQuade took a notion to track him he wouldn't catch up too fast. Boag was hoping Captain McQuade would come to the Santa Cruz to find out how Boag's war was going. But he didn't want Captain McQuade's army showing up before the fight started. Anyhow it was a distant hope at best; he couldn't count on Captain McQuade coming and even if he did come it didn't mean he'd help out.

It was about seventy miles up the ridgebacks of the Sierra Madre to the Santa Cruz district and it took Boag all day and half the night to get there, and that was pushing hard; the wagon horse was all used up by the time he stopped in the middle of the night. He got on his saddle horse and rode around the town of Coronado, following Jackson's directions, and at about two in the morning he found the wagon road that had to head up to the old mine that Mr. Pickett had turned into his fortress.

He stopped along the creek bank and dipped a canteen of water out of the stream; he set it down on the ground long enough for the floating debris to settle to the bottom before he drank out of it. He looked at the night sky; he didn't see many clouds but he could smell a change in weather coming and he tried to work out ways to make use of it.

The ruts of the old road had once been worn right down to bedrock but years of disuse had filled them in here and there with enough topsoil to grow weeds. In places the weeds were belly high on Boag's horse. But they were limp because they'd been crushed down lately by the passage of wagonwheels and they hadn't sprung back fully. Heavy wagons, Boag judged. Possibly Mr. Pickett's big vault, coming up the road in sections.

It was good country up here, a lot of timber and meadows. But when Boag reached the edge of the forest and looked up the road he could see why Mr. Pickett had chosen the spot. It was a *mesa*, a tabletop mountain with a steep cut running up into it for the road—possibly it was a natural cut because it would have taken a prodigious amount of blasting to man-make it. From the parapet on top of the mountain the sentries would have a clear command of almost a mile of cliffs and open flats. You couldn't get anywhere near that mountain without being spotted; not on this front approach at least.

Boag turned the horse to the right and began to ride a full circle around Mr. Pickett's mountain.

He kept inside the fringe of the trees because he didn't want them to spot him. The route took him along a ragged line, bulging and doubling back with the trees, so that it consumed most of the remaining hours of the night. He found that the trees came up reasonably close to the bottom of the mountain on its back side, to the north, but that was no use because the cliff was too sheer to scale. The mountain was shaped like a stump, as if it had once been the base of a tree forty miles high. Ridges ran out from its base like the roots of a stump and some of them climbed pretty close to the top; but there was always at least twenty or thirty feet of sheer cliff above the ridges, and there was a man-made stone wall above that, and he was sure the rawhiders had rifles in the gunports up there. By the time he got back to his starting point at the foot of the wagon road it was nearly dawn and he hadn't seen any way in or any way out except for the road cut. Mr. Pickett had got himself a choice spot.

Boag thought of a few ways he might smuggle himself inside, aboard one of Mr. Pickett's arriving wagons for instance, but the idea didn't have any real strength to it. You didn't go into the enemy's camp when he had you that badly outnumbered.

The main purpose his tour had served just now was to confirm an expectation: Mr. Pickett had found himself a fortress that was damn well nigh impregnable.

But it was also damned hard to escape from. It could nicely be turned into a trap.

A prison for Mr. Pickett?

The idea made Boag grin for a while but in the end he gave up on it. He had no patience for a siege and it would be practically impossible for one man to keep that road bottled up for any length of time. A man had to sleep some time. All they had to do was wait him out and slip past him when he slept and stick a knife in him.

Boag had made a kind of a plan before he'd ever seen this place. Now that he'd reconnoitered and discarded a couple of alternative plans, he saw that his original plan was still the right one.

It was the only one, in fact.

You didn't go in after the enemy. You made the enemy come out to you.

By sunup he was riding back around the perimeter of Coronado town. He got back to the wagon where he'd left it, hitched up and drove the wagon back along the same route to the forest that aproned Mr. Pickett's mountain. Well back inside the trees where they couldn't see him, and off a hundred yards to the side of the road, he stopped the wagon and walked out to the edge of the trees to get a view of the ground and pick his spots.

There was a long ridge that came down the western side of the mountain and sloped into the trees, breaking up into a number of tributary ridges and hogbacks and canyons. It might do; but the military axiom was not to fight with the sun in your eyes and if he set things up there, he'd be at a disadvantage in a morning fight. Boag might be able to influence their actions but he couldn't force them to pick a time of day that was convenient to him. So he discarded that area and looked for another.

Trees gave a man good cover and it had occurred to him he might set up right alongside the wagon road itself. But there were too many corridors through a forest. You needed a spot where the numbers of routes and accesses was limited. Otherwise you couldn't enfilade them all.

This was Thursday, about the middle of the morning, and he didn't know for sure when the first of Mr. Pickett's gold bearers would arrive but from what Jackson said it looked as if they were all due to show up some time tomorrow. To be on the safe side he gave himself until midnight to set up.

He got the saddle horse and rode a little way around the south perimeter. It took him more than an hour even though he was covering only a few dozen acres, mostly because he had to keep out of sight wherever he went but also because he had to be patient, he had to take his time and pick the best possible spot if he was going to have any chance at all of making it work.

Once he thought *Why the hell am I doing this?* But he didn't dwell on it; he was keyed up and ready for the battle and at times like this you didn't think about why, you thought about how. Working out the methods took all a man's conception.

"Hey now."

He said it to himself very softly and with considerable satisfaction; he backed the horse a couple of strides and mused upon the scene.

It was mostly cutbanks and rocks. The ridge came sprouting out of the base of the mountain and meandered its way south into the trees, and at this point there was a gravel-bedded dry creek with here and there a dried pool caked with cracked mud. Several groins led into it, like the fingers of an outstretched hand. Once you entered any one of the little canyons you were restricted by the high sharp-cut banks, confined pretty much to the creekbed while you rode upstream into the central canyon of it. A man might be able to climb out of it but a horse couldn't; the sides were twelve or fifteen feet high and the rushing waters of rain-season flash-floods had eaten the banks away until they were not merely vertical cliffs, they were mostly undercut so that the tops overhung the gravel bed and shadowed part of it. Pine roots made tangles sticking out of the washed-away banks; a man could climb up that way, hanging onto the roots, but he'd make a hell of a target while he tried it.

Boag ground-hitched the horse and walked up into the little badlands. He kept his feet on the pebbles where he wouldn't leave easy tracks. He walked several hundred yards up the canyon, following its twists; when he looked back he couldn't see farther than the last bend. Overhead the forest crowded close along the top of either bank. In places the washouts had knocked the nearest trees over; several logs lay in the creekbed and a few deadfalls spanned the canyon like bridges. It was maybe forty feet wide.

At the head of the canyon there was a wall of limestone that had been eaten flat and discolored by flooding. You could see that in times of heavy rain it became a waterfall. Right now it simply boxed in the head of the canyon. It wasn't prohibitively high; the waters had worn it down and right now a man sitting on a horse could just about see across the top of it. But his horse wouldn't make the jump up onto it because the footing underneath was too soft: it was silt that had washed down in the floods and caked into a treachery of clots and pits.

Boag had about a quarter mile of canyon to work with. At this back end there was the box formed by the waterfall. A the other end, facing Mr. Pickett's mountain but hidden from it by the pines, a half dozen sub-canyons splayed out from the main cut, and the whole thing got gradually absorbed into the system of wrinkles and heaves that the big mountain had at its feet.

"It'll do," Boag decided.

He went back to the wagon to get the big coil of wire.

7

It took him the whole day to make the place ready. He took his time because if you did it just a little bit wrong you could find yourself getting trampled to death by twenty horsemen. He had no way of knowing how much of a crew Mr. Pickett had with him up there but the size of the fortress implied a substantial phalanx of them and it was for certain that Mr. Pickett had all the money it took to hire as many gunmen as he wanted.

Picking the site for the Gatling gun came first because everything else had to be tied into that. He finally set the thing up on its swivel tripod at the top of the outside bank of the first bend below the waterfall. From here he could fire down into a hundred-yard length of the canyon and he could also swivel the gun around to cover the fifty yards between here and the waterfall. It gave him full command of the entire box end of the canyon and you couldn't do better than that.

The next thing was to make a ladder that would get him from the creekbed up onto the bank. He used a fallen log for that and trimmed the branches until he had just enough knobs left on it for footholds. Then he jammed it securely at the bottom.

He had to decide on the placement of the tripwires. Not too far down the canyon because that would give them the opportunity to scramble back around the bend, behind cover, invulnerable to the Gatling gun. So he strung the wires not more than fifty feet downstream from his gun position. It meant they would be perilously close to him and if a few of them got through they might swarm right up the bank and overrun him; but then there was another way of looking at it: the closer they came, the harder they'd be to miss.

He tied the wires taut; his anchors were the exposed roots that stuck out of the cutbanks on both sides of the defile. He strung the wires at two levels. The first rank of them hung about six feet off the ground where it would catch a man right across the chest and knock him off his horse. The second rank he placed ten yards closer to the gun position; he strung them lower, just a couple of feet off the creekbed where they would trip the horses.

He thought about it a while and then he strung eight or ten wires across the canyon at both levels because if the light was good enough for shooting it would be good enough for men to see the wires; they would duck under the high ones if they had the chance but if there were enough wires it would be like a spiderweb, they wouldn't get past all of them.

He counted the kegs of blasting powder. Four of them. Not enough.

"Well you don't need to knock down the whole canyon, Boag." He rummaged through his packs and found a can of coffee, which he emptied and filled with blasting powder, and Jackson's canteen which was a spare now; he filled that too. He could make a couple more charges simply by packing the powder under rocks. The rocks would make good shrapnel but of course that wouldn't work if it rained even a few drops. It didn't *look* like rain but there was a feeling of weather in the air, a dampness that got into his nostrils and made his injuries creak.

He buried the charges in the banks and in the floor of the canyon. One of them he put in the ground at the bottom of the canyon wall just beneath his gun position; he relied on the overhang to protect him from the blast and he wasn't planning to set that one off unless things went bad and they swarmed too close to him.

The next thing to do was to make damn sure they stayed down in the canyon where he wanted them; it would get uncomfortable if they got over the banks. Even the ten-barrel gun wouldn't chop down trees and if they got behind him he'd be finished. He had to prevent that; he had to keep them down in the creekbed where they'd be as exposed as a baby's butt.

He did it with trenches and a log. He measured the log to make sure it would span the canyon from the Gatling gun to the far bank. He cut a deep groove in the log from end to end and he laid it across the gorge like a bridge, with the groove side up like a flume. Then he scratched trenches from both the near end and the far end of the log; the little trenches were maybe a foot wide and six inches deep and they ran down an easy pitch along the crests of both banks, all the way down to a point near the approach bend where the creek bottom had a wide rock depression in it. He fed both trenches down into that dry pool. Then he tested it by pouring water from his canteen into the grooved log.

The water ran across the log and followed Boag's trench along the far bank. There wasn't enough water in the canteen to get all the way to the dry pool, but he saw it would work and that was all he needed to know.

He wired the blasting charges with fulminate-of-mercury detonating caps and wedged the caps where he could see them from the gun position. You couldn't string a fuse that long; some of the charges were nearly a hundred yards from the Gatling. He had brought the kerosene and the lassos because he'd expected to unravel the ropes, soak them in kerosene and use them for fuses; but that wasn't going to work and he would have to explode the charges by shooting at the mercury blasting caps. They had to be in plain sight.

But now he had a better use for the kerosene and he might find a use for the ropes too.

The last thing to set up was the rifles.

There hadn't been any .38-56 in camp but Captain McQuade had got him a .40-90 repeater and Boag would keep that for his saddle gun; it had enough wallop to knock down a horse and enough range to do it at four hundred yards if you were good enough to hit what you aimed at that far away. Boag was good enough. He still had to sight it in, but that would be later.

The rest of them were assorted rusty junk. Mostly rolling-block carbines, a few old rifles. One Springfield single-shot .45-70. He plugged a cartridge into its trap-door breech and loaded the rest of them and went around looking for places to put them.

Most of them he tied fast to trees with pieces of rope. He aimed them generally down into the canyon. They weren't supposed to hit anybody, they were just supposed to make noise. He tied them very firmly and ran wires from their triggers to the Gatling gun position. Then he went around cocking them all and reminding himself not to trip over any of the God damn trigger wires.

Finally he made hand bombs by packing fistfuls of blasting powder tight into two saddlebags, a gunpowder pouch, and the horns of a cow skeleton that lay bleached at the edge of the trees. He melted down his candle and sealed the horn bombs with wax that had frayed bits of rope sticking out for a fuse. He put all these things except the saddlebags into his pockets and made sure the sulphur matches were handy in his shirt pocket; he checked the box of .40-90 cartridges and loaded the repeater's magazine full and rammed the rifle into the saddle boot. He still had three revolvers—the two he'd stolen from guards in the Ures jail and the one he'd taken off Jackson's partner—and he loaded them all with six cartridges and dropped the hammer pins between the rims. With the seven in the repeater's magazine it gave him twenty-five shots without having to reload. That ought to make enough noise to stir them up a little; it was all he needed.

He ate his meager supper sitting by the Gatling gun in the twilight and considering the setup, trying to think of what else to add, trying to decide whether he'd made any mistakes. If it was going to work at all it had to work completely; he couldn't afford any casualties to his army because if they ever got near enough to put one bullet in the right place the whole war would be over.

After he ate he rode two hours back into the mountains and found an open stretch along the side of a razorback ridge with a southwest exposure and enough light for him to sight in the long rifle. He used up thirty rounds satisfying himself with his knowledge of it, where its bullet would fall at fifty yards and where it would fall at two hundred and roughly four hundred, and then he bellied down and got a good steady hold and laid his cheek against the stock to squeeze off four shots at a full paced-off five hundred yards.

He walked it off to see where the shots had landed and found that they had all punctured the log within a circle that he could span with the brim of his big Mexican hat. The circle was a couple of feet higher than he'd expected it to be; he put that bit of information back in a part of his mind where it wouldn't get lost.

He cleaned the rifle and built a little fire. He had retrieved the lead from a few of his practice shots and he had a bar of lead from Captain McQuade; he spent an hour melting and molding and crimping, reloading the cartridges he had fired.

Finally he rode back to the foot of Mr. Pickett's mountain. His legs hurt like fire and he was rocking with groggy fatigue; it was weak in his muscles and gritty in his eyes, the burning starvation for sleep.

He lay back and went limp, eyes drifting shut.

chapter eight

1

The first gold bearers showed up on the wagon road in the middle of the morning and Boag was ready for them.

There were three of them and a pack horse. They must have been riding all night; they looked half asleep in the saddle. The same detailing of men Mr. Pickett had employed back in Arizona, Boag noticed—two reliable old rawhiders and a young Mexican gunman festooned with pistols.

Boag had strung wire across the wagon road down in the weeds where nobody was going to cotton to it in advance. The two riders hit the wire abreast and when their horses stumbled and went down on their chins the Mexican plowed into the tangle because he and his horse both were too sleepy to react fast enough.

Boag pulled the overhead rope and the blankets dropped on them.

The blankets fell curling like fishing nets. The looming shadows terrified the horses. Boag dodged a panicking horse and stepped out of the trees on the edge of the road with cocked .45's in both hands. The three rawhiders were batting at the blankets and Boag found the outline of a hatted head under a blanket and swatted it with his gun barrel. There was a moan from under the blanket.

The Mexican pawed clear and spotted Boag but Boag was close enough to make it suicidal and the Mexican just put his hands up in the air. Boag whipped around behind him and shucked the guns out of the Mexican's holsters and when the third rawhider crawled out from under the tangle Boag had a bead on him.

"Don't get notions now."

The rawhider blinked in baffled incomprehension. His sleepy brain hadn't caught up with the things that were happening to him. "What the fuck?"

"Gun belt off," Boag said.

The rawhider had to absorb it and stare at Boag for a minute before he squeezed his eyelids tight and popped them open as if to clear his head. But Boag was still there and the rawhider nodded bleakly and disarmed himself.

Boag kicked the blanket off the third one, the one he'd hit on the head. The man was on his knees bent far over with his head almost touching the ground; he was holding his head in both hands and rocking back and forth in pain.

Boag said to the Mexican, "Get him on his feet and bring him."

He prodded the three of them back into the woods to the little clearing where he'd left the lengths of cut wire. "You. Wire the Mexican's hands behind his back. Do it tight, I'm going to check it."

When the three of them were wired to trees too far apart for them to reach each other, Boag went after the scattered horses.

He kept listening for the approach of more riders. He didn't know how close they'd arrive together; he was expecting to have to let some men get by him but he meant to intercept as many as he could.

He'd seen the pack horse bolt to the north; that was the only animal he was really interested in. He rode that way looking for sign and found plenty of it; the horse had crashed through the forest in blind fear but naturally it hadn't kept that up very long. A quarter of a mile back in the woods he found the horse grazing.

He led it back to his little clearing and tied it up. Had a quick look at the gold and checked the lashings on his prisoners. He didn't answer any of their questions or threats. He went back to the road and hiked up the blankets and tightened the tripwires and waited for the next bunch.

2

He had nearly a two-hour wait. He heard them coming; one of them was whistling *Dixie* and it made Boag's lip curl.

Only two of them this time, a team like Jackson and Smith: a fat one and a thin one. Otherwise they had the same stamp of the other rawhiders: the short-brim Border hats, the double-cinch Texas saddles, the flannel shirts and beat-up Levi's and scuffed Missouri boots and the same hard half-shaven faces. As they came up the road he recognized Sweeney, the one who was whistling.

When they hit the wire he dropped the blankets on them and stepped out into the road with a .45 in his fist. With his free hand he grabbed the lead-rope of the pack horse.

He couldn't find a head to beat on; he just waited for the rawhiders to get untangled.

Sweeney's partner rolled out from under the blanket; he'd been hurt—maybe hit by a horse's hoof. Boag watched him for a second and then holstered his gun and bent down to pluck the man's gun from his holster. The man didn't even notice; he'd been clipped on the elbow and was holding it cupped in his other hand, rolling around in a silent agony, too hurt to scream.

Holding the man's gun Boag turned to look for Sweeney and found him coming up from the blanket trying for his gun.

Boag would have been dead there if Sweeney's fall hadn't hitched his gun belt around. The holster was somewhere behind Sweeney's butt and he was still trying to find it when Boag cocked the revolver and leveled it.

"Quit that, Sweeney."

"You."

"Yeah me. Unbuckle that thing and leave it drop."

So now he had five men neutralized and two pack-horse loads of gold.

When he got Sweeney and his partner wired up to trees in the clearing he rigged up the blankets again and inspected the wires. One of the tripwires had snapped and he replaced it.

Assume these loads were the same size as the one Jackson had cached. If all the gold was split up this way, there'd be maybe six more loads on the way in. But most likely Mr. Pickett had already spent some of it and had kept some more. Mr. Pickett had got a lot of paper scrip from Don Pablo of course and he'd probably used that, rather than the gold, to pay off the corrupt officials of the Pesquiera regime; but he wouldn't have let all the gold out of his reach. Boag expected that if he managed to shanghai two more loads it would do the job; three more would guarantee it.

He got another installment somewhere around one o'clock. Two riders again, the pack on a mule this time. One of the horses got through the first line of tripwires but fell over the second line. The blankets were getting ripped up by now and one of the men showed an inclination to fight but then like the others he discovered he was looking into the black orifices of two steady forty-five caliber muzzles and he thought better of it. You didn't fight the drop; that was a first rule of anything.

That made seven prisoners and close to a hundred-thousand dollars U.S.

It was a lot of hard men to be leaving off by themselves in the woods. He kept re-checking their wire lashings at close intervals because it only took one loose wire to bring all seven of them down on him.

He made a cache of all their weapons and kept it close to his position by the side of the road. Most of their saddle horses had drifted off somewhere and perhaps some of them would wander up into Mr. Pickett's fortress. That was all right, that was fine. He wanted Mr. Pickett to get nervous.

Mr. Pickett had to be nervous by now anyway. No gold had showed up yet. Mr. Pickett was going to get angry and worried.

That was part of the idea.

He hadn't bothered to try putting gags in his prisoners' mouths. Right now they could yell all they wanted to; nobody except Boag was going to hear it. They wouldn't have any way of knowing when their friends were approaching—he had them tied up beyond earshot of the road—so they couldn't warn the approaching gold riders. There wasn't much they could do with their mouths right now except complain.

Then at half past two he was in trouble. He could see them coming up the road toward him and they were too many. Five men and two pack horses.

Obviously it was two groups who had met on the way in. They'd joined up and now they were spinning yarns happily and Boag didn't see what the hell he could do about it because in one minute they were going to hit the tripwires.

3

They were strung out along a forty-foot patch of road and when the leading pair of riders hit the tripwires Boag dropped the blankets on them and spun his guns onto the other three, stepping out in plain sight and talking loud:

"Now freeze. Right now."

But it was no good, they were fighting men and they'd been ambushed before; they were yanking reins and ducking before the words were out of Boag. Boag shot one of them out of the saddle and dived back into the trees and their guns opened up; Boag wheeled behind the pines and saw one of the rawhiders lift his leg over, light on both feet and fire from a crouch under the horse's belly. The bullet hit the tree right by Boag and drove wood splinters into his left hand; he almost lost his grip on the revolver.

He answered the shot but the horse got in the way and he heard the horse scream; the man was dodging into the pines.

The other one was somewhere in the trees on the opposite side of the road; Boag could hear his horse crashing through the brush. The pack horses were still in the road, rearing.

Boag moved ten feet through the trees and put his attention on the tangle of blankets and horses and men in the road where he'd netted the first two; the men were getting out from under it now and the shooting had told them what was happening. Boag got down on one knee and laid the right-hand pistol barrel across his left forearm and when the first man batted out from under the blanket Boag shot him in the chest.

The other one came out shooting, throwing the blanket off him in violent rage. But he made the mistake of looking at his wounded partner and that gave Boag plenty of time. Boag's first shot hit him somewhere in the upper chest and the second one a little lower.

He still had one on each side of the road, both of them in the woods.

Boag moved fast. He didn't care about the noise because the rawhiders were just as deaf as he was now: you didn't hear much of anything for a little while after firing off guns close to your own ears.

He went back into the woods looking for the one he'd last seen afoot. The man would be advancing on Boag's roadside position; Boag got away from there as fast as he could and then began circling back so that he might come up behind his stalker.

He'd fired five out of the right-hand gun. It was one of the revolvers he'd taken off a rawhider; he had four of them stuck in his belt. It was a Smith & Wesson .44 and he had no more cartridges for it so he dropped it and drew out a .45 and slowed his swing through the trees now; he kept swiveling his head fast to pick up movement in the forest shadows but he couldn't see anything stir and his ears were still jangling from all the hard racket.

This was when you got fully scared. There just wasn't any way to know when the other fellow would spot you and take a bead on your back.

Then he spotted the movement. Back close to the road; the man was moving up the road just inside the trees.

Boag didn't run after him; Boag settled down on one knee and took steady aim on the spot where the man would next appear.

But the man was too smart for that; in a stalk fight you never traveled in a straight line, it gave the enemy a chance to set you up in advance. The man never showed up in that hole in the trees and Boag was back where he'd been before with two of them out against him.

A horse broke through the trees with a lot of noise; there was an instant when the noise stopped abruptly and all Boag heard was the thunder of hoofbeats, and then the crashing started up again and subsided as the horse slowed down.

He knew what it meant. The man on the far side of the road, the one still on horseback, had made his run to get himself back onto this side of the road. So now they were both here in the woods not far from him.

Then over the ringing in his ears he heard dimly the call of a man's voice which quickly became a chorus of yelling.

That was Boag's seven prisoners back in the clearing, calling to their friends.

It gave Boag his solution; he broke into a run.

4

Watching the horseman approach, Boag held his fire. He wanted both of them in sight.

He had a stitch in his ribs; he had run like a son of a bitch all the way to the perimeter of the clearing. He'd stopped there in a jungly tangle of brush where the seven prisoners couldn't see him. They were still bellowing for help and Boag let them go right on yelling; they were a beacon for the two rawhiders to home in on. It would draw the rawhiders and Boag would wait for them.

It had worked with the one on horseback. Boag saw him stop the horse a hundred feet away and scan the forest with patient care, gun up. If he came too close Boag would have to nail him but he wanted to wait for the other one, the one on foot.

Boag's legs felt as if they'd been attacked by a red-hot cross-cut saw. He was in no condition for sprinting; practically a cripple and here he was trying to outrun a horse. The whole damn thing was madness. . . .

He saw the horse stir and he watched out of a corner of his vision while the horseman proceeded cautiously toward the yelling. Boag put most of his attention on the woods to his left because that was where he expected the dismounted one to show up.

The shifting shadows were uncertain; twice he thought he saw something but it turned out to be branches roughed up by the breeze. Grey clouds were drifting over the woods and starting to mass; there might be rain later on and he didn't want that, it would soak all his blasting powder apparatus. But there was no time to worry about that.

He let all the air out of his lungs and whooshed in a massive breath and held it a while before he exhaled all of it and filled his chest again close to capacity. It was an old trick he had learned; it kept you from panting after fast exertion. It wouldn't do to be all out of breath when you had to have a steady aim. But the big black body was beat-up and he didn't have the reserves he'd had before the injuries; blood flowed in his eyes and pulses throbbed all through him. He couldn't tell how well he was going to be able to shoot even if he wasn't out of breath.

The horseman was taking his time, moving forward a few

yards and stopping to keen the forest, then walking the horse a few paces and stopping again to search. When he got a little closer he'd spot Boag easy.

There was no more time. Boag locked down his aim the best he could; he'd just have to hope the shot didn't pinpoint him for the other man in the woods.

There was a red haze across his eyes and the gunsights wouldn't hold still. He took a huge breath and let some of it out and held the rest in his chest; he gripped both hands on the revolver's handle and laid his right thumb up along the recoil plate the way you did on the handgun range at Fort Lowell but it still wasn't enough; the pulsebeat made the muzzle jump off target every time. He felt like an old man with palsy and he got very angry with himself.

The horseman slowly lifted his right leg across the saddle-horn. He was going to drop to the ground and proceed on foot. Some sound arrested him that way and he sat precariously on top of his saddle, turning his head in a slow half circle trying to figure out what had alerted him.

He was looking right at Boag when Boag squeezed the trigger. The explosion startled Boag, as it should; but he knew he'd missed and when he went to cock the gun he saw the rider gather himself to dive off the saddle. Boag emptied the gun as fast as his thumb would slip the hammer; the shots roared like a string of giant firecrackers.

One of the bullets hit the rider somewhere, not mortally; he spilled awkwardly to the ground and started to crawl. Boag pulled a fresh gun and poured the whole cylinder at him in desperation.

The man fell flat with his gun splayed out from an outstretched hand but Boag still wasn't confident he'd hit him again; the man could be playing. Boag dropped the two empty revolvers and pulled his last pair and moved through the trees, approaching the downed man by stages, keeping near cover and watching the whole world for a sign of that other man.

The man on the ground began to struggle with his elbows and toes, trying to crawl. He was hit pretty bad but Boag got twenty feet closer to him and deliberately shot him twice, killing him, because a dead man wouldn't get up behind him and shoot him.

When the bullets started spraying at him the only thing that saved Boag was the thickness of the timber. Branches deflected the first ones—he heard them scream viciously—and by that time Boag's sluggish reflexes caught up and he was diving into the brush, curling himself behind the bole of a pine mindless of the twigs that raked his face and hands and laid his skin open.

He saw the faint muzzle-flash of the sixth shot and felt the tree jar a little when the bullet slammed into it. He knew where the man was but there was no point answering the fire; underbrush would do the same thing to his bullets that it had done to the rawhider's.

It was one of the few times in his memory that Boag wished he had his hands on one of the .45-70 Springfield carbine single-shots that every soldier in the Army hated. The big ball of lead would cut through any amount of brush and keep right on going until it hit something big enough to stop it.

But all he had was a pair of revolvers and two legs that were giving out on him, and blurred vision and a sense that the last cards had just been turned over and he'd lost the game.

5

He squatted with one leg bent to run. His eyes still weren't focusing properly. He could hear Sweeney and the rest of them calling out to the rawhider: "He's right over here, man."

"Shut up Sweeney," the rawhider yelled from out in the woods. "I know where the hell he's at."

"That you Billy? Listen come untie us, we'll hep you hunt."

"Just shut up your mouth a minute," Billy called angrily.

Boag got down on his belly and crawled.

He moved six inches at a time. He knew where Billy was but he couldn't get much closer than this without exposing himself; the only chance was to bring Billy to him. He crawled in a fairly wide circle around the clearing where Sweeney and the rest of them were sweating in their wire manacles; he hitched himself around to where he'd tied up a few of their saddle horses that he'd caught when he was chasing after the pack animals. He stood up then and looked around, rubbed his eyes and looked again; nothing to see, not yet anyway. They couldn't see him from the clearing or they'd have been yelling the news to Billy.

Boag removed the bridle from one of the horses and used it like a whip; he bellowed at the top of his lungs as if he were riding the horse:

"Hyaah, hyaah! Giddap!"

The horse ran away with a racket and while distance was absorbing the sound Boag eased closer to the clearing and flattened up behind a tree where he could watch.

"Hey Billy I think he give it up. Get your ass on over here and turn us loose."

But Billy didn't come right in; he didn't accept it that easily. Boag heard him moving, though. After a bit he decided Billy was making a circle around the clearing to make sure it was all right before he walked into the open.

Boag was waiting for him when Billy came in sight. Boag's gun was cocked and so was Billy's but the difference was that Boag's was aimed at a target and Billy had to swing his around through a short arc, and it gave Boag enough of an advantage in time: Boag's slug rocked Billy's head back and Boag could see by the way he fell that Billy was dead.

Boag slid down with his back against the tree until he was sitting on the ground. He couldn't stand the pain in his legs any longer; he sat there and wept silently.

Presently he became aware that Sweeney and the rest of them were yelling.

"Hey Billy, what the hell's happening? Where you at?"

"Hey come cut us loose God damn it."

"What the hell you doing back there, shooting at shadows?"

"He's lit out, Billy. Come turn us loose you son of a bitch!"

Boag gathered his feet under him and limped into the clearing. He stared at them out of the depths of his red eyes and after they all quit caterwauling he said, "You might as well shut up now," and he forced himself to hobble back toward the road.

6

He stood in the road looking up toward Mr. Pickett's mountain. He felt like shaking his fist.

Nobody was coming down the road from the mountain yet. But they must have heard the shooting up there; they'd think about it, they'd worry about it. They'd put it together with the fact that none of their gold had showed up yet. They'd have to keep picking at it until they found out, and the only way to find out was to come out of the fortress.

They were taking their time because they had no way of knowing it wasn't a whole goddamn army down here ambushing their gold riders. They'd be talking it over up there, Gutierrez and Ben Stryker and Mr. Pickett; they'd be up on the parapet right now with field glasses trying to see something down here. Maybe they were looking at Boag right now. It was too far for them to see who he was or even what color he was, even with field glasses; but they'd see a man standing out in the road looking up at them and they might think he was a bandit or a rebel soldier who had a vast army back in the trees.

It would deter them from coming right down after him. They'd want to stay put behind their parapet where no army could get at them; all they had to do was keep their guns on the road cut and they could slice a whole army to pieces a handful at a time as it advanced through that narrow gorge. Rifles up on the parapet would cut down every man.

Boag wished he knew how many guns Mr. Picket had up there.

His legs were trembling under him and the pains lanced into him every half second. Something had busted loose inside his hip. He couldn't walk ten feet without almost collapsing.

Spittle ran from the corner of his mouth. He wiped it away in great rage and stumbled off the road into the woods to get a horse. He spent a good five minutes hoisting himself into the saddle but once he got aboard he knew it would be all right. It hurt like hell but he wasn't going to fall off.

It took nearly an hour to round up the two pack horses. He tethered them with the other three. Counting the gold he'd taken out of Jackson's cache back in Tres Osos he had close to two hundred thousand dollars' worth of Mr. Pickett's bullion and that was the lion's share of it; there might be another pack horse or two still coming in today but Boag had enough. He dismantled the tripwires across the road and threw the torn blankets away in the woods. He saved the wire.

He spent the afternoon moving everything to his Gatling gun site. He lashed the prisoners' guns to trees, pointed down into the gully, and wired their triggers to his gun position; it made for a couple dozen guns, all cocked and ready to be fired from his command circle. He tied the five pack horses together on a picket line and fixed the ends of it to trees with bow knots because he might have to move out very fast and he wanted to be able to take them along with him.

One at a time he cut the prisoners loose of their moorings. He stood them up, not unwiring their hands, and tied them all together on a short-hobbled picket wire, and moved them slowly up to the cutbank gully where he was going to fight his little war. He separated them and wired each of them to a different tree, and sat down to eat.

He sat there until midnight because his legs weren't going to move him anywhere. He cleaned the .40-90 rifle again and found he wasn't having much success convincing himself the game was still worth the risk. He'd had good luck a couple of times today, without which he'd have been dead, and it was all the luck he was likely to get. He had half the money in the world; he'd taken it away from Mr. Pickett. What more was there to fight about?

Sweeney kept ragging him in a twanging voice and finally Boag got mad enough to gather his wobbly legs under him and go over and clout Sweeney across the head. After that they all kept their wretched thoughts to themselves and Boag sat down to do some more thinking.

The thing was, it hadn't done Mr. Pickett the kind of harm he was going to feel. He'd lost a pile of gold but he still had some of the bullion and he had all that money he'd taken off Don Pablo. If the point of all this was to bring Mr. Pickett down, Boag hadn't accomplished it yet.

And that *was* the point of it. He no longer knew why, but it was.

You got past the point where you needed reasons. All Boag could remember now was that back in the beginning there had been a reason for it. It had been a good enough reason then, whatever it was. Probably it was still a good enough reason but he didn't have the strength to seek it out in the recesses of his head.

A lot of times you made a snap decision and then had to live by it for the rest of your life. Back on the Colorado River a lot of miles ago Boag had made a decision and on account of it he had almost got killed God knew how many times, and when you had risked that much for something you didn't quit even if you could no longer remember what the risks were in aid of.

So there was only one thing to do and there wasn't any point arguing with himself about it. The war was started and it had to be fought through to its finish.

He needed rest. He needed a month flat on his back. But right now he was beyond it. Time to rest now would be time to fall apart. He had to keep moving. He limped to his horse and checked the hand bombs and checked his rifle and his matches and his revolvers, and he climbed up into the saddle as if it was a high mountain and rode out toward the wagon road.

7

He got halfway out to the road and realized he'd made a stupid mistake. It changed his course; he rode back to the Gatling gun and made gags out of blanket strips and wads and forced the prisoners' mouths open and inserted the gags and tied them around behind their heads. He told each one of them the same thing:

"Don't fight this gag too hard. You make yourself sick, you could strangle to death on your own vomit. Hear?"

Then he left them. It was harder getting on the horse this time. He almost didn't make it.

He stayed just inside the trees and went up alongside the road to the edge of the timber. From here it was just about a mile to the top of the mountain. Most of it was across a steady, open slope and then there was the high cliff that was sliced in half by the road cut.

There still wasn't any way to approach unseen. But this time Boag wanted them to see him.

He had one gold ingot on the saddle. He had a dime novel he'd taken off Sweeney. He had a bullet. He had some coiled pieces of wire. These were all he was going to need tonight but he had festooned himself with weapons just in case.

He ripped the back jacket off the dime novel because the inside of it had no printing on it. He used a bullet for a pencil and wrote out a short message in heavy lettering. He couldn't spell worth a damn but Mr. Pickett would be able to read it all right.

He wired the note on top of the gold bar.

Then he put his horse out of the trees and rode straight up the wagon road toward Mr. Pickett's mountain.

He had to assume they were watching; they'd be fools not to.

They were watching him ride forward and wondering who he was, whose side he was on; they wouldn't shoot at him and even if they did it was a hell of a shot to make because he only went as far as the foot of the road cut. He looked up at the high cliffs on either side of the cut and he couldn't see anybody silhouetted up there but that didn't mean anything; they'd be there all right. The sky was matted with clouds anyhow, he wasn't too likely to see them unless they moved; they'd blend with the rocks.

He tossed the gold brick right out in the middle of the road. He turned his back to the mountain and rode back toward the forest, but he didn't go the whole way. About two thirds across that distance he stopped and turned the horse around to face Mr. Pickett's mountain.

It was well beyond rifle range of the mountain; well beyond rifle range of the foot of the cut where he'd dropped the ingot.

He made his seat as easy as he could on the saddle, and he sat there the rest of the night waiting.

8

It was daylight—a grey mottled sky—before they sent a man down into the notch to find out about the gold brick. Boag watched the rider approach it cautiously. They hadn't been sure it wasn't some kind of bomb; that was why they'd waited for daybreak to have a look at it.

The rider dismounted and picked up the brick and got back on his horse and rode up the cut. Boag watched him disappear over the top of it.

He sat there patiently, knowing they were watching him from the mountaintop. They'd be thinking about it. Mr. Pickett would read the note two or three times and try to make out what it meant.

MR. JED PICKETT
I GAT YOR GOLD, HEAR IS PROOF.
YO COME DOWN AND WE TAWK ABOT IT.
I AM WAITING WAR YO CAN SEE ME.
—BOAG, FRMRLY SGT USA.

They would be thinking about that and trying to estimate how big an army Boag had with him back there in the woods, and they would be trying to work out ways to get their gold back.

They had the same limitation Boag had. He couldn't get into their fortress without being seen, but they couldn't get out of it without Boag seeing them. They had to come straight down the road cut.

Boat waited them out. He had no place to go. He ate dry beef and took a swallow from his canteen.

He saw some of them moving around on the parapet; he could almost see the gun muzzles stir. He counted five moving figures.

He dismounted and lay down flat to ease his cramped legs; he kept the reins in one hand. He crushed his hat into a pillow so that he could keep his head propped up far enough to watch Mr. Pickett's mountain.

One big worry he had was the sky. It was really clouding up for rain.

He saw them come down from the parapet on horseback. While they were still in the shadows of the rock gorge he rolled over onto his knees and gave his attention to the problem of getting onto the horse. He punched his hat out and put it on, and put the reins in his teeth and lifted his left leg with both hands to get his boot into the stirrup. Then he let his foot hang there in the stirrup while he wrapped both big fists around the saddle horn and hauled himself up by the strength of his arms. He let his right leg flop over the saddle and while he felt for the stirrup with his toe he kept his eyes on the mountain and counted the riders who were emerging from the bottom of the cut half a mile away from him.

Sixteen, seventeen. . . .

Twenty-three of them in the end. He had no trouble recognizing Ben Stryker's big frame swaying on the saddle of the leading horse.

It was about twice as many as he'd expected but he didn't trouble himself about it. The shape Boag was in, all it would take would be one or two of them, if they escaped the trap.

When he set it up he'd been convinced it could work. But now suddenly he was picturing all the things that could go wrong with it. He knew there was no way to win, not against twenty-three of them.

And Mr. Pickett wasn't even with them; he'd stayed up there in his fortress.

Boag gathered the reins in his left hand. *I could grab those gold horses and make a run*, he thought, but he had less than a half-mile lead now and they'd ride him down in ten minutes.

It was no time to change his mind. He had no choice.

He turned his horse to the right and lashed it to a gallop, running along the flats parallel to the edge of the forest. Behind him he saw Stryker's crowd veer left to cut across the triangle on an interception course.

He eased closer to the trees, still at a dead run; he reined in after a quarter mile and wheeled the long .40-90 out of the boot and put it to his shoulder. He wanted to sting them beyond hesitation so he put the whole magazine into their midst and he saw one horse go down; he doubted he'd hit any men but you couldn't expect much accuracy shooting from the saddle.

He lifted the saddlebags off the horse, the saddlebags he'd packed with blasting powder. He lit the hanging fuse and dropped the saddlebags on the ground and cut back into the trees.

Low branches whipped at his face. He laid himself flat and rammed on through. He reached one of the fingers of the cut-bank gully and galloped into it just as he heard the explosion behind him. He wondered if any of them had been near enough to get hit by it; it was doubtful.

He was galloping full out and the hoofs were throwing a lot of dust in the air and it would still be hanging there when Stryker reached that point. Boag wanted them to know where he was; they had to follow him.

He took big breaths and held them deep and long, storing up oxygen for the coming climb. Those old battered legs had to make one more effort, that was all; he willed it into them.

Riding fast through the bends he finally came in sight of the Gatling gun and he could see vaguely on either side the rifles aiming down from the brush above the banks.

He stopped the horse and ran through the tripwires and got onto the log ladder he'd made; he started to climb but his legs just weren't going to make it.

"God damn it Boag," he muttered through his teeth. He pushed and shoved and forced his legs to lift him and when he rolled onto the top of the bank he reached over and hauled the log up after him so they wouldn't be able to follow him.

Then he emptied the hand bombs out of his pockets and dropped the .40-90 beside the Gatling gun. Yanked the corks out of the kerosene jugs and poured the fluid down the trenches he'd dug, and into the log that flumed across to the far bank.

Over his own hard breathing he heard the angry hammering of the approaching horsehoofs.

Just don't let them stop to think.

He emptied the last jug and felt around for his oilskin pouch of matches.

He found the sulphur tips and then Stryker was drumming into sight in the bend.

Boag dropped flat on his belly behind the Gatling gun and hoped he had enough brush piled around so that they wouldn't spot it too soon.

The riders came in like Cavalry at full charge and it was good to watch: Boag felt the skin tighten around his grin.

They hit the tripwires and Boag lit a handful of matches and threw them into the kerosene trenches. The horses tumbled and flipped and began to scream. One rider vaulted out of the saddle and his horse went right over on its back with a bloody foreleg dangling broken.

Kerosene flames raced down the trenches on top of both walls. The fire leaped a yard or more in the air and made a bright stockade fence along both banks. Boag felt the sudden dry heat of it.

Up in a crouch he swung the Gatling onto them and began to wield the firing crank. The gun set up a steady chugging stutter of fifty-caliber fire and he saw the rawhiders and Mexicans wheeling and yelling in confusion. Some of them had been unseated and some had dismounted voluntarily and a few were still on horseback trying to find something to hide behind but the racketing yellow flames rushed past them and around behind them.

When the fire hit the creekbed pool at the bottom behind the rawhiders it went up like explosives with a roaring bellow of ten-foot-high flame. Most of the kerosene had run down into the pool and collected there and it was better than a solid wall of entrapment because it not only contained them, it drove their horses to madness.

Boag yanked on wires and his fixed rifles opened up into the gully floor, shooting from all directions through the yellow flames.

The banging of rifles and the stink of kerosene smoke filled the rawhiders with panic; there was no sense of organized defense down there, they were all scrabbling frantically in circles and the smart ones were digging in behind the corpses of horses which in most cases they shot themselves to create parapets. He saw Ben Stryker's head rise up behind a dead horse and turn quickly to survey the ambush and Boag picked up the .40-90 but by the time he fired Stryker had dropped out of sight. Boag swiveled the long sights toward the glisten of a mercury cap ten yards to the left of Stryker's position; he fired twice and the second bullet hit the cap and set off the blasting charge.

Stryker disappeared under the explosion of sand and clay, horse and all.

Boag sighted on another blasting charge in the far bank. It brought tons of cutbank clay down on two crawling men.

He found another blasting-cap to shoot at and it went off right under a horse. Boag saw the rider throw up his arms and begin to pitch from the saddle before the rising cloud of sand absorbed him.

He jammed a new magazine into the ten-barrel gun and swiveled the muzzles and worked the crank. He saw the bullets make spouts in the creekbed; he corrected the aim and sewed a stitch of bullets across a tangled knot of men.

It was the most confined concentration of battle Boag had ever experienced and he had never known anything like the stink and earsplitting racket of it.

Boag kept moving as fast as his arms would work. He pulled more rifle-trigger wires, he shot another blasting charge that blew up like a geyser and knocked four men over, he raked the gully with an X-pattern of Gatling fire.

Ben Stryker had pawed his way out of the dust; Boag heard him yelling somewhere in the smoke, summoning men, trying to organize a rush on the Gatling gun position; Boag tried to find him but the cloud of sand and smoke was billowing through the length of the gorge and he could hardly see the opposite bank.

He pulled trigger wires and discovered these were the last rifles; he had fired them all now. There were no mercury caps left to shoot at except the one immediately beneath his gun position. The kerosene was making more smoke now, the flames shrinking; he had vague glimpses of flitting motions through the gully. He counted the remaining Gatling magazines—two loaded ones, fifty rounds in each; after that he would be down to his sidearms.

He had made a lot of noise and violence but he hadn't done enough real harm to destroy their effectiveness: maybe he'd killed five of them and maybe ten but there'd been two dozen men to start with and at least half of them were still shooting at phantoms through the roiling smoke. Ben Stryker's heavy voice rolled through it all and Boag knew they would charge him quickly now. When they did they would probably overrun him. They weren't fools; they'd come at him from both sides at once and he couldn't cover both directions simultaneously with a Gatling gun or anything else.

So it was time to cut and run. That was what the small voice told Boag.

He never did listen to that voice.

He knew how it had to go; he had to get away clear and he couldn't do that with a dozen of them still armed and on their feet right behind him. He had to put Ben Stryker out of the way and most of Stryker's old rawhiders. The Mexican hired guns he didn't care about because they were only in this for gun wages and when they thought their side was losing they'd get themselves away. They had no loyalty to Mr. Pickett. But Ben Stryker and the rest of those old timers wouldn't quit until they were dead.

It had a chance of working because it wasn't the Mexicans who would have the stomach for a head-on charge. Nobody would follow Ben Stryker except the old hands. That was why Boag didn't run. He stayed put and waited while the smoke began to settle and when he saw the first bunch crawling toward him, close under the overhang of the near bank, he swung the Gatling gun that way and held it silent until they were good targets through the patchy smoke and then he opened up as fast as he could swing the crank.

As soon as the gun began to stutter the rawhiders split up and went running at full sprint in a crazyquilt of directions that looked lunatic but made sense: they were scattering to charge from all directions at once.

Boag swept the gun back and forth in a half circle and saw three of them go down but they were coming too fast from too many angles and he wasn't going to be able to hold them.

When the magazine ran empty he didn't reload the Gatling. He put a match to the fuse of his canteen-bomb and heaved it toward the bunch that was closest to him, the bunch sliding along the near wall; he didn't wait for the explosion, he swung his revolvers onto the farther group across the gully and while their bullets whined off the barrels of the Gatling gun he aimed under its belly and slammed bullets into them. While the bomb exploded and rained sand on him, the .45's bucked and roared in his fists; he fired alternately right and left even though he had always been an indifferent left-handed marksman.

They were closing in at the foot of the bank beneath him and the barrels of the Gatling gun wouldn't depress that far even if he still had ammunition in it. That had been Ben Stryker's plan all along: get underneath the ten-barrel gun's field of fire and attack from below.

They were going to scale the bank by clinging to roots. Boag could see the sweat shine on their oily faces: five of them and Ben Stryker coming up fast from the left.

Boag fired a .45 into the blasting charge he had buried at the foot of the slope.

The explosion knocked him back on his left arm. It blasted the Gatling gun off its tripod and the damn thing fell across Boag's butt like a tumbling safe.

He couldn't tell if he was hurt and it was no time to stop and find out. He heaved the thing off him and scooped up a revolver and dragged himself forward on his belly to look down over the blown-up lip of the bank.

Four of them had got it. One had nearly been blown in half; three lay asprawl; the fifth one was reeling away into the smoke holding his ears.

The rolling echoes of the explosion still caromed down the canyon. And Ben Stryker was still coming at him from the left but Stryker hadn't seen Boag yet and Boag lifted the revolver and took a good bead on him.

He never knew why, but at the last instant he pulled his aim. When he fired he put the bullet deliberately into Ben Stryker's shoulder. It was a .45 with point-blank velocity and it knocked Ben Stryker clean off his feet and hurled him out onto the gully floor.

The Mexicans were shooting fast, bullets were all over the woods and Boag got the hell out of there.

9

In the woods he stopped to make an inventory of his bones.

All the articulated functions seemed to be in fair working order. But his legs felt like jagged stakes that somebody had driven up into his hips with a hammer.

He would have been worried by that if they hadn't felt exactly the same way before the explosion.

He was stone deaf and didn't know if it was temporary or if the concussion had cracked his eardrums, but he found no blood in his ears and that was a fair sign.

He came by the clearing where Sweeney and the others were gagged. They watched him with round red eyes.

They could be trouble. If he left them alone and somebody cut them loose there were plenty of guns lying around to arm them with. He had no way left of fighting them.

But he hadn't much option. He wasn't gaited to shoot all of them cold.

He'd just hope to be away from here by the time they got loose and organized.

He went right past them and didn't stop to talk. He was traveling light now; he had one of the hand bombs left and he had the .40-90 rifle in his fist and two .45's in his belt. He remembered his promise to Captain McQuade about the Gatling gun but first things had to come first. He cinched up one of the rawhiders' saddle horses and unfixed the pack horses' picket line and rode back into the woods leading the string of gold-packed animals.

It would take them a while to quit fighting shadows back there. There were maybe ten Mexican gunslingers and a couple of Ben Stryker's rawhiders left unhurt, and maybe half a dozen more with injuries. Ben Stryker would be too busy keeping himself alive to worry about revenging himself on Boag, and the Mexicans had probably lost the belly for a fight. Most of them would scatter and go looking for other smoky jobs. Ben Stryker might find his way back up the mountain sooner or later with Sweeney and those others, and Mr. Jed Pickett would spend however long it took to find Boag and kill Boag and get his gold back.

Therefore this was not the time to take the gold and ride away. There was one thing left to do.

Boag hid his tracks and cached the pack animals and at the end of the cloudy afternoon began the slow ride back up the road toward Mr. Pickett's mountain.

chapter nine

1

There was rain.

It came down steady and gentle in the night; it matted the shirt to Boag's wedge-shaped back. It was a friend and Boag thanked it.

He left the horse at the foot of the gorge and walked up the road cut. Mr. Pickett might have a lookout posted up there but it wasn't going to do him any good, nobody was going to see Boag walking up the road in this. A black man in dark clothing at night in a rainy canyon? Boag had to feel his way and twice he tripped over big boulders he hadn't seen.

Not far along his legs began to give out. The climb was not terribly steep—it had been designed for the passage of heavy wagons—but it had not been built with bullet-crippled legs in mind. Several times Boag had to stand still while spasms of agony wrung him out and all his muscles knotted up in cramp. The weight of the gold brick in his left hand increased steadily and so did the weight of the long rifle in his right.

He kept climbing, taking his time. Toward the top the light became fractionally better and he could vaguely make out the box shape of the *hacienda* and the darknesses of several outbuildings and the workings of the old mine. The rain slanted steadily across the mountain and little gullies ran down the road past his boots.

If there were sentries they hadn't seen him. They'd have heard a horse approach; that was why he'd had to accept the anguish of the climb.

There were no lamps burning anywhere. Mr. Pickett wouldn't be that stupid.

Boag moved slowly and without sound. He reached the corner of the dark house and tipped his head back to look up. Rainwater runneled out of the trough of his sombrero and splashed down his back. He didn't blink at the drops that hit his upturned face.

A narrow staircase edged its way up the outside wall; wooden handrails ran up both sides of it. There was a landing at the top, a door, a row of windows with rain beating on the panes.

Boag walked around the *hacienda* and found the horse barn attached to the side of the house. He slipped inside with caution; there might be a stable keeper.

He found nobody. He counted eleven horses but what was more interesting was the saddle count. Three wooden pack saddles and five riding rigs, of which two were Texas saddles and the other three Mexican. It was doubtful anybody who came this far to work for Mr. Pickett would be without a saddle of his own; so it told Boag what he wanted to know about the size of Mr. Pickett's force up here.

Mr. Pickett, Gutierrez probably, and three others. It stood to reason. Mr. Pickett had committed most of his force to his second in command for the attack on Boag's shadow army. Greed for the gold had made them take that risk.

Boag saddled up one of the horses with the big Texas stock saddle that was probably Mr. Pickett's own. Boag enjoyed the idea. He found a bridle, working mainly by touch, and when he had the horse ready to go he spent a very bad ten minutes getting himself up into the saddle.

In the ticking silence of the flooding night he ducked low to clear the barn doorway and rode out of the stable. He walked the horse around the front of the house and stopped it square in front of the big adobe steps that went up to the main doors. There were windows beside the doors. Boag tested the weight of the gold bar in his hand. There was no note tied to this one; there didn't need to be. Boag hurled the brick through the window and before the clattering of crashing glass had subsided he was moving at a gallop toward the head of the road.

When he hit the top of the sloping cut he was half sure he heard a door slam back there.

Somebody yelled at him from out on the cliff but Boag kept going right down the road.

2

From the edge of the trees he watched the dawn pink up Mr. Pickett's mountain.

What was it going to take to make them mad enough? Boag had waited all night in the pouring rain and they hadn't stirred from the mountain. When the rain stopped and the first premonition of dawn came, Boag had moved back from the foot of the mountain to the forest and continued his vigil from there.

But finally they came. Because it was easier to act than to wait.

Boag watched them ride down the cut. Five of them. The big buckskin horse in the lead, that had to be Mr. Pickett.

Boag put his horse out of the trees, showing himself. He had rehearsed the whole thing in his mind during the night, over and over again, and there was only this one way to do it.

He rode straight toward them, not hurrying; the horse had an easy-gaited walk. Mr. Pickett reached the bottom of the cut and came trotting out away from the foot of the mountain, staying on the road, coming right down toward Boag with his four outriders in a pack right behind him. There was no dust in their wake because of the six-hour rain.

The ruts were a little muddy and Boag put the horse along the side of the road in the grass, still walking it. His eye measured the distance as it closed between him and Mr. Pickett. The stretch from the base of the mountain to the edge of the trees was almost exactly a half mile; so he had distance yet to cover.

They would watch him coming and assume he wanted to talk; they would have heard all the tumult and thunder of battle yesterday and they would know by Boag's appearance that Ben Stryker had been whipped, and they would have to assume that Boag had a lot of guns covering him from the edge of the forest behind him. Still they had come down to see what he wanted—and to kill him if they could.

Boag stopped his horse about two hundred yards out from the woods. He did that because it was what Mr. Pickett would expect of him. He was staying within easy rifle range of the pine forest, where his "army" of rifles could cover him.

Mr. Pickett came on at a grinding deliberate trot, not hurrying it up and not slowing it down; moving forward like an engine.

Regardless of what Mr. Pickett believed about the army behind Boag, the fact was that there was Boag on one side and five of them on the other. His plan didn't have much chance, not really, because once the ruckus began they'd realize quick enough that Boag was all alone out here.

But there weren't any alternatives that made sense so Boag just played it out.

They came along and then they stopped about halfway out from the mountain. The low sun was behind Boag's right shoulder. In its light the ground fog lifted gently off the dewy meadowland and the breeze made ripples in the shining grass. Mr. Pickett sat on his horse a little better than a quarter of a mile away, not moving, and Boag knew he was too far so he gigged his horse and advanced at a slow walk with both hands resting on his saddle horn like a man who wanted to talk a deal.

Mr. Pickett put his horse in motion again and now Boag recognized Gutierrez behind him and a rawhider who went by the name of Hooker, riding bareback. The other two were Mexican gunslingers with rifles across their saddlebows.

His eye kept ranging the distance. *Four-fifty*, he estimated, and he let the horse carry him on closer to them.

Four hundred. All right now.

He steeled himself against the pain and made his moves in quick synchronized coordination. Turn the horse crosswise to the road. Stop the horse. Loop the reins over your left forearm. Lift your right leg over the cantle behind you and step down onto that right foot. Pull the left boot out of the stirrup and set it firm on the ground a couple of feet away from the right boot. Lay the .40-90 across the saddle. Aim.

They were in motion of course but he wanted Mr. Pickett only, he didn't care about the rest of them; and they weren't moving so very fast because they didn't credit anybody with much luck at four hundred yards' range. That was one thousand, two hundred feet and a lot of things could happen to a bullet in that distance, starting with the inaccuracy of the shooter.

It was Gutierrez who fired the first shot but that was from the back of a moving saddle and Boag ignored it. He had Mr. Pickett in his sights. Mr. Pickett was yanking the horse around to the left and Boag gave it the lead he thought it needed and squeezed the shot, holding both eyes open and maintaining the focus of his vision not on the target but on the front sight of the rifle because that was the important thing to watch.

The bullet went home. He knew it had, but Mr. Pickett was still on the saddle out there and the horse was still wheeling. Gutierrez had overcome his surprise and was ramming away to come in at Boag from a circle; Gutierrez was flat on top of the horse, making a low silhouette, firing a left-handed revolver at Boag merely as a diversionary thing, not expecting to hit. Boag had to ignore it, had to keep his sights on Mr. Pickett while he jacked a fresh shell into the chamber and settled the sights and waited for his God damned horse to still its feet. If he lost his horse he'd have to get down on the ground to shoot and he'd never get back up on his feet again so he kept the reins wrapped tight around his forearm and spoke softly:

"Gentle down, now. Gentle down."

Mr. Pickett was riding in a dazed circle and one of the Mexicans was leaning over to reach for the reins of Mr. Pickett's horse. Boag shot Mr. Pickett again and this time it did the job. It knocked Mr. Pickett off his horse.

The Mexicans split in opposite directions and broke into dead gallops. They weren't giving it up, they were doing what Gutierrez was doing: attacking circularly. In the meantime Hooker was stopping his retreat to find out what had happened.

Gutierrez was closest and it was Gutierrez Boag picked on.

But Guttierrez was down flat across the withers and Boag only knew one way to handle that. In the Cavalry you had it drilled into your bones.

Shoot the horse.

He gave it a lead and squeezed, and missed completely.

But there was time. The next one took the horse somewhere in the forequarters and it shuddered, breaking stride in mid-run, and when Gutierrez fell off the saddle Boag had the clear view he needed.

But Gutierrez came up with revolvers snapping and Gutierrez was damned good. Boag felt a half-spent slug ram into the horse; Boag was firing then and he got his shot off but when he went to jack the rifle the horse just slid over against him and Boag had to windmill back away from it before it fell on him.

That's all then. He was standing right out in the bare-ass open with no shooting rest, and Gutierrez was out there wounded but still shooting and the two Mexicans were circling in and now Hooker, riding bareback, was barreling straight down the road at him.

3

He didn't have to stop and calculate the loads; he was a soldier, he always knew how many rounds he had left. There were two in the magazine and one in the chamber.

Gutierrez was out there in the grass reloading his revolvers. Two hundred yards and he'd downed Boag's horse with a six-gun.

But Gutierrez had a slug in him and he was afoot. He wasn't the one to worry about.

Boag did the only thing possible. He laid himself down behind the dying horse and braced the rifle along his left hand and watched Hooker drum straight at him and shot Hooker spinning out of the saddle.

The Mexicans had galloped out in a V to straddle Boag's position. He picked the one to his right because the other one was getting close to Gutierrez's position and at least that would put the two of those where Boag could watch them both at once.

The rider to his right was going at a dead run on a course straight across Boag's line of vision. That meant he was moving fast and Boag gave himself a long lead before he fired. It was three hundred yards or better and he was bleakly unsurprised when the bullet did nothing visible. He used the last shot and that one missed too, and then he slid down flat on the ground and wondered as he thumbed cartridges out of his pocket if he had time to reload the long gun.

4

When Boag looked up, the Mexican on his right was within forty yards of the trees behind him. It left Boag no time at all. He leveled the rifle, only four cartridges loaded so far, and jacked it and aimed with painful slow care and squeezed it.

A little too much of a lead but it creased the horse on the forehead; at least that was the effect Boag observed. The horse's head snapped to one side under the impact and the Mexican made the mistake of trying to get the horse under control when he should have jumped clear. It gave Boag time to sight on a fairly motionless target and in two shots he had the Mexican.

Back to one bullet left. He swiveled toward Gutierrez and the other Mexican and reached for cartridges.

There wasn't anything in sight but a riderless horse wandering away.

He knew what it meant. The Mexican had dismounted somewhere near Gutierrez and they were both out there in the grass, worming their way toward Boag.

He didn't know how bad he'd hit Gutierrez. He knew he hadn't hit the other one at all. And he knew one other thing: he was at the end of his capacities and he had no strength for a drawn-out stalking game. They would shoot him to pieces before he had time to react.

Boag didn't care about them now. He wanted to get out.

He had one of the hand bombs left but it might have got too wet last night to work. He might as well try it. He opened his packet and struck a match, got the fuse sputtering and hurled the thing as far as he could into the grass on a line with Gutierrez's horse. It didn't go more than sixty feet. All he hoped for was that it would make noise and encourage them to hesitate.

But it didn't go off, so that was that.

He took the rifle and eeled into the grass. It would be sensible to crawl back into the woods. That was what a smart man would do. That was what Gutierrez and the other one would expect him to do.

So it was what Boag didn't do.

He headed up through the grass parallel to the road. Heading straight up toward the foot of the mountain.

Because that was where Mr. Pickett had fallen and Mr.

Pickett's horse was still standing there waiting for his rider to get back up and ride him.

5

The wind rubbed itself against the damp grasses. Boag's legs were all gone now and he was hitching himself along on his elbows with the rifle across the crooks of his arms. He'd left his sombrero behind and the sun beat against the back of his head. That was all right because he was wet and chilled clear through and the warmth was comforting.

He doubted there was any flesh left on his elbows. He lifted his head and saw the norse wasn't far away now. Another fifty feet to cross.

He found Mr. Pickett almost by accident; he parted the grasses and there was Mr. Pickett lying on his side looking right at him.

There was a heavy smear of blood glistening on Mr. Pickett's shirt. His face bulged, thick with blood and anger; the pulse throbbed at his throat and he worked his lips around a word:

"Boag."

"You keep quiet now, Mr. Pickett. This bullet comes out your back it'll make a hole as big as a coconut."

Mr. Pickett just stared at him.

Boag thought of a lot of things he ought to say to Mr. Pickett. All the agony that had led up to this. But there wasn't anything left to say, the guns had said it all. Boag brought himself around until he was lying parallel to Mr. Pickett and then he used his arm to sit up. He looked out across the waving grass. Nothing stirred except the grass itself. They were still there but he had the feeling they were nowhere near him.

He lowered himself onto his side and rolled his knees

under him. When he sat up again he was kneeling. Mr. Pickett just watched, neither moving nor speaking.

Boag balanced himself on one knee and hauled his left leg up, knee against chest, placing the left foot flat on the ground. All his nerves twanged with taut pains. He braced his left palm against the upraised knee and pushed himself upright, dragging the right leg up under him until he was standing there precariously, bent double, one hand on his knee and the other on his rifle.

When he began to walk it was like the movement of a puppet. His legs jerked around loosely under him. He had to get balanced on one foot and then drag the other one forward a few inches, rearrange his weight onto it and repeat the process.

He made his way around Mr. Pickett and Mr. Pickett's head turned to watch him. Mr. Pickett seemed to have lost his guns. His holsters were empty; there was no rifle in sight.

His eyes were fixed on Boag with single-minded concentration; they never even blinked.

Boag reached the horse. It shied away from him and he shuffled toward it again and hooked up the trailing reins in his left hand. He turned to look at Mr. Pickett.

"If I leave you to heal, you'll come after me, won't you?"

Mr. Pickett made no response of any kind.

Boag said, "I ought to shoot you now."

But he slid the rifle down into Mr. Pickett's saddle boot. It was not impossible getting himself aboard the horse because he used his arms to pull himself up, but swinging his right leg over was the hard part. He had to pull the leg over with his right hand. It took him a while to get his toes into the stirrups.

Mr. Pickett had laid his head back and was lying that way, looking up at Boag with the back of his head on the ground. Boag said, "You come after me I'll have to kill you next time."

He eased the horse closer. "You hear me, Pickett? I got your gold but don't you try to do to me what I done to you. You ain't as good a fighting man as me."

Pickett's raw eyes just stared.

Boag leaned down a little. "You hear me Jed Pickett? I'm a better man than you are. You hear?"

It was not clear whether Pickett heard or not. Somewhere in those few moments he was dying. When Boag moved out on the horse the dead man's head did not turn to follow him; the eyes kept staring at the sky where Boag had been.

Somewhere out there in the grass or the trees Gutierrez and that Mexican were still moving around but Boag was all finished here. He made a long ride along the base of the mountain and entered the trees a mile east of the road. He would go by the gully and see about the Gatling gun. If it wasn't occupied by Ben Stryker's people he'd retrieve it for Captain McQuade but he wasn't going to fight for it; he'd only told Captain McQuade he'd return it if it was possible, and fighting was no longer possible today.

Miguel and the *señora* stood in the doorway and watched the coach come across the hills. It was a handsome brougham drawn by matched teams of greys and it stopped sedately in front of the villa. A liveried coachman climbed down from the driving seat.

Don Pablo came softly out into the sunshine and Dorotea touched his sleeve. The coachman opened the ornate door of the brougham and Dorotea lifted her chin.

Boag stepped to the ground, putting his weight on a gold-headed cane. He had a cigar in his mouth and a tailored grey suit on his back.

He said to Don Pablo, "The dowry's in the coach."

"You are alive, *mi amigo.*"

Dorotea said, "You will stay here now?"

"I'm going up to Arizona to look for a little girl that goes by the name of Carmen."

Don Pablo said, "Of course you will take Dorotea with you," and turned back inside the door because it was too hot for him out here.

Boag handed his hat to Miguel. Dorotea gave him a suspicious and dubious eye. Boag said, "That would be up to the lady."

"The lady will think about it," Dorotea said.